A VERY BOSSY CHRISTMAS

ALEXIS WINTER

"SWEETHEART, I KNOW EXACTLY HOW TO HANDLE YOU."

Those eight little words whispered in my ear by my boss were my undoing.
And what we did after he said them, most definitely landed me on Santa's naughty list.

Let me back up...
If there's one man who can suck all the joy out of Christmas—it's my boss, Damon Wells.
I should have known when fifteen minutes into our first interview, he told me that nothing about me stood out from the fifty other applicants.

Yet somehow, I'm sitting shotgun in his fancy sports car on the way to my family's house for the week.

You'd think he'd show a little mercy this holiday season after my day from hell.
Car towed? Check.
Spilled coffee on my white blouse? Check.
Soaked in Chicago slush by a cab? Triple Check.

Instead, he threatens to fire me.

So now I'm stuck spending the holidays with my *boss* by my side…Until two minutes into meeting my family, Damon introduces himself as my boyfriend and my minor panic turns into a full fledged five-alarm holiday meltdown.

He wasn't supposed to pretend to be *anything*.
He absolutely wasn't supposed to stick his tongue down my throat when he promoted himself to fiancé in front of my entire family.
And I sure as hell wasn't supposed to enjoy it.

Suddenly, our fake little fairytale is starting to feel too real when Damon slides my grandmother's diamond ring on my finger.
The same ring I thought my ex was going to give me last year when he dumped me.
The same ex who shows up to my family's holiday party.

All I want for Christmas this year?
To forget just how good my boss is in the bedroom before my heart starts to get other ideas.

Copyright © 2021 by Alexis Winter - All rights reserved.

In no way is it legal to reproduce, duplicate, or transmit any part of this document in either electronic means or in printed format. Recording of this publication is strictly prohibited and any storage of this document is not allowed unless with written permission from the publisher. All rights reserved.

Respective authors own all copyrights not held by the publisher.

PROLOGUE
KATE

"Come on. Come on. Come on."

I hold back tears as I turn the key for the fourth time, praying the engine turns over this time. The car whines loudly over and over again as panic builds in my chest.

"Of all fucking days." I can't hold back the tears that prick my eyes any longer as I pound the steering wheel. I stare at the blurry clock as big tears tumble down my cheeks. I wipe at them desperately as I realize that not only am I going to be crazy late for work and face a sharp tongue-lashing from my asshole boss, but now I have to figure out how I'm going to get my car fixed in time to drive home for Christmas.

I look over at my passenger seat to the large pastry platter and two coffee cartons that should have already been on the conference table ten minutes ago. I feel bile build up in my throat as I picture the giant vein on my boss's forehead about to burst.

My thoughts are interrupted by the shrill ringing of my phone and I glance down to see his name plastered on the screen—Damon Wells. "Speak of the fucking devil," I mumble as I swipe the screen to answer.

"Mr. We—" I start with my most chipper voice but I'm quickly interrupted by his enraged bark through the phone.

"Where the hell are you, Miss Flowers?" he hisses. "The partners are all here, sitting around the table waiting for you with the goddamn breakfast food and reports. Surely you can't be so incompetent that you can't handle picking up some pastries. Hmm?"

He's whisper shouting at me and I can picture him pacing, running his hands through his hair in exasperation as he pinches his nose dramatically. It's his classic temper tantrum demeanor, something I'm very used to at this point in our professional relationship.

"Mr. Wells, I can explain. I have the coffee and pastries and I'm on the way. I ju—"

"Get here in ten minutes or you can pack your shit!"

"I—hello? Mr. Wells?" I pull the phone away from my face and see that the prick hung up on me.

"Ahhhh!" I scream in my car, wanting nothing more than to punch Damon Wells in his perfect white teeth. I'm sure it's deranged but the thought of seeing his bloody mouth and watching him flip backward over his desk gives me more glee than I care to admit. I should probably get back into therapy. I would if I could fucking afford it working for Mr. Tight Wad.

I look at my phone; there's no way in hell I can make it in ten minutes but I have to try. I grab the tray of pastries and two cartons of coffee while trying to hold my purse and hail a cab. I trudge through the dirty slush of melted snow that has now filled my high heels as I step to the curb and raise my hand. I manage to get a cab quickly and pile into the back seat as I rattle off the address to the office.

"If you could hurry, please, that would be great." I offer the most genuine smile I can muster but the driver just ignores me. I reach into my wallet and look at the cash I have; I'll be lucky if I have enough to cover the fare and maybe give him a few dollars for a tip. I don't even have enough to bribe him with an extra five dollars to step on it.

I stare at my phone the entire way. We're less than half a mile away when I get a taunting text from my boss along with a picture. I open it, confused at first to see the image.

"What the—?"

Damon: *Two minutes, Miss Flowers. Look, I was even nice enough to grab a box for you.*

The image shows a large box on my desk. "What a fucking sicko!" I say loudly, causing the driver to look up at me in the rearview mirror. "Oh, sorry, sir. Not you. Just my... never mind." I pull the wad of cash out of my wallet this time and stare at the meter. Looks like I have just enough to cover it. He slows the cab down in front of my building and before he's even stopped, I throw open the door.

"Whoa, lady. Hold your damn horses!" he shouts.

"I don't have time!" I yell as I scramble out of the cab with my bag slung over one shoulder, the pastries in the other, a coffee jug in one hand and one under my arm. I go to hand him the cash that I've tucked under my chin when I drop one of the coffee jugs.

"Shit!"

"Crazy woman," he mutters as he takes the cash and speeds away.

I pick up the jug and inspect it briefly; it's one of those cardboard containers so it appears undamaged. I tuck it back under my arm, holding it tightly against me as I scramble to the front doors.

"Hold it!" I yell as I sprint through the lobby toward the open elevator doors. I'm breathing heavy, doubled over, and laughing that I made it. I glance at the watch on the guy next to me and see I have thirty seconds to spare.

"Hey, you're, uh—leaking something?" The man says as he takes a step away from me. I glance down to see what he's looking at and see that coffee is running down my leg and pooling onto the elevator floor. In my rush, I didn't even feel the warm liquid soaking through my blouse.

"No, no, no!"

"Good luck." The doors open and the man steps out without even offering to help me.

"What the fuuuuuck?" I yell as the doors close and reopen a moment later on my floor.

I scramble through, running down the hall and flinging open the conference room door. All twelve shareholders turn their heads to stare at me. I can feel Damon's eyes attempting to burn a hole through me, but I don't give him the satisfaction of making eye contact. I feel like I'm in a fucking Drew Barrymore movie. I'm sweating; my hair has half fallen out of the clip that's holding it up, and I'm now soaked in coffee and still dripping it down my leg. I don't even care; I'm at my actual wit's end.

Without a word I toss the pastries on the table along with the still full coffee jug before spinning on my heel and marching back to my desk.

"Miss Flowers!" I can hear the stomping of his Salvatore Ferragamo shoes as he marches toward me.

"What in the actual fu—"

"Not a fucking word." I spin around and shove my finger in his face. I can feel my body shaking as I ball my other hand into a tight fist. I'm praying he goes off so I have an excuse to finally pull back and sucker punch him.

Instead, he puts his hands up and takes a step back, noticing that my white blouse and pale-pink skirt are now stuck to my body with coffee.

"Whoa, what happened to you?"

"Seriously?" I snap.

"My car died this morning outside of the bakery while I was picking up your precious fucking pastries. Then you called and bitched me out and didn't even give me a chance to explain what happened and that I needed help. Instead, you threatened me and so I used the last of my cash on hand to hail a cab with my already full arms and then dropped one of the coffee containers because I sprinted to get up here so that I didn't lose my job." I can feel my eyes bulging out of my skull as I work to keep my voice steady. "So now I'm soaked in coffee and I have no way to go home and change."

He takes another step back before straightening his tie. "That sounds like a helluva morning, Miss Flowers, but you'll just have to clean up as best you can and then bring those reports into this meeting that is now"—he looks at his watch disapprovingly, like it somehow has offended him too—"thirteen minutes behind schedule. I can stall for another five minutes, but that's all you get."

I'm about to lunge over my desk now and rip him apart like a defenseless gazelle on the Serengeti in the clutches of a merciless lion when he turns and starts to walk back toward the conference room but then stops abruptly.

"One more thing. If you could maybe ask one of the other ladies in the office if they have a spare set of clothes, that would be great. Can't have my secretary looking like she got hit by a bus and dragged for a few blocks, now can I?" He laughs.

Yup, I'm going away for homicide.

I manage to get myself cleaned up as much as I can before walking back into the conference room with the stack of reports. The rest of the morning speeds by in a blur and I'm counting down the minutes till I can go check on my car and retrieve my coat that I realize I left in there this morning.

"Hey, Marge, I have to run an errand so I might be a few minutes late getting back from lunch."

"Mr. Wells okay that?" she mutters, not bothering to pull her face away from her computer screen.

"I'll hurry," I say which is neither a yes nor a no, but Marge is a snitch and I don't have time to ask dickweed for permission. I rush outside, clutching my purse tightly against me as the cold Chicago wind whips around me and goes straight to my bones. I have to take the train to the station closest to the bakery I was at since I don't have the cash for another cab ride. I get off on my stop and briskly walk the three blocks to Crumbs and Caffeine.

"Where's my car?" I glance around the street, double-checking I didn't just walk past my own car, but no, my car is nowhere to be found. I feel my throat tighten but I choke back the immediate response to burst into tears. "There has to be an explanation," I say as I glance around frantically. I'm about to step into the bakery to see if they know anything when I glance up at the signs on the pole in front of me.

Something people might not know if they aren't from Chicago is that street parking is like a sick game the city likes to play on us residents. Not only are there multiple signs on the pole outlining when you can and can't park, but there's also exemptions like if it's a holiday, a weekend, your mom's thirty-third birthday if it lands on a Tuesday and there's more than a ten percent chance of rain.

"Oh my God, this literally cannot get any worse." I pull at my hair, laughing hysterically to keep from sobbing. I draw a few stares from weirded-out onlookers who probably assume I'm in the midst of a complete mental breakdown—they're not wrong. I take a few deep breaths and read the signs again, noting the name and number of the towing company. I punch the number in my phone and wait for an answer.

"H&R Towing, this is Jake," a guy's voice booms through my speaker, his over-the-top Chicago accent making him sound like a character from a movie.

"Yes, I parked outside of Crumbs and Caffeine by Halstead and West Jackson and I think you guys towed my car."

"Yeah, ma'am. You can't park there. It's fifteen-minute parking." I bite my fist, reminding myself not to snap at him; he didn't do anything wrong.

"Mm-hmm, yup, found that out. So do you have a 2009 Kia Optima at your lot? Silver, plates are KITN 78." I hold my breath as he clicks around on his computer.

"Yup, looks like she's here. It's a fee of one seventy if you pick it up today. We're open till five."

I rub my forehead. "One hundred and seventy dollars? But you guys just took it a few hours ago." I can hear myself getting to that whiny place and I take a few deep calming breaths.

"Sorry, ma'am. Policy. It's one fifty the moment we hook it to our rig and then twenty a day lot fee for the first five days. Goes up to thirty-five a day thereafter."

"I, uh—" I scramble trying to figure out how I'm going to make this work today when I can't leave work till five thirty at the earliest. I took tomorrow and Friday off to drive home and be with my family since Christmas is next week. "Did the car start, do you know?"

"We don't have the keys, ma'am." I look down at my purse and realize I'm an idiot for asking that question.

"Okay," I say, my voice shaking. "Thanks, I'll figure it out and try to get there today." I slide my phone back into my bag before raising both hands toward the sky. "Why me?" I yell just as a cab comes screeching into the open spot in front me, spraying me with slush from head to toe.

I don't move. I'm literally frozen from my lack of coat, the now-melted snow all over me, and the utter shock of what this dumpster fire of a day has turned into.

"Hey, lady, you getting in or not?" the driver yells at me. I just stare at him, or stare at my own reflection in the rear passenger window of his car. You can see through my blouse that is now a lovely shade of brown from the coffee and dirty snow; my mascara is running down my cheeks, and my hair looks like roadkill on my head.

The driver flips me the bird before driving off, leaving me to drag my ass back to the train station.

I

DAMON

What in the actual fuck is she wearing?

I can't help but gawk at Kate's getup and not in a good way. The brown wool skirt she has on looks like it's at least four sizes too big and cinched at her waist by a rubber band wound around the excess material gathered at her back. If the skirt wasn't enough, she's paired it with a turtleneck that's a different shade of brown. She bends forward, leaning over the desk to show Marge something. The skirt might be fugly as hell, but it still looks delicious draped over her perky ass.

Even though four out of five days a week I want to wring Miss Flowers' delicate neck, I'm still a man, and that woman has a body that is nothing short of a fantasy. It's probably good her personality instantly kills my raging hard-on whenever she walks into my office; otherwise, I'd probably have had to fire her. Can't have my assistant falling in love with me, thinking our hookup meant a marriage proposal.

"You're going to end up in HR." Teller, our sales director, nudges my elbow and laughs.

"Nah, she prefers to take her wrath out on me in more fucked-up ways than that." I don't take my eyes off her. Something Marge said has made her laugh and I watch as a genuine smile spreads across her lips. A small pang of jealousy hits me in the gut when I think about the fact that I've never made her smile. Not even once.

"You're lingering," he says, looking between her and me.

"Yeah, and?"

"Someone's got a crush." I flick my eyes back to Teller as he wags his eyebrows.

"A crush? What is this, junior high?" I scoff.

"Just saying, you don't just lust or leer when you look at her... You linger."

"What's with you, man? Charlotte have you watching those Hallmark movies again?"

"Laugh all you want, buddy, but they get her all emotional, and then I get to comfort her and she's so appreciative of my sensitive side that she ends up getting all hot and bothered, and then we make our own Hallmark movie, if you know what I mean. Sex, we end up having sex."

"Yeah, got it, Tell." I turn my gaze back toward Kate just as she's standing back up and walking over to her desk. She doesn't notice me at first but then our eyes meet. For a brief moment, it feels like the air has been sucked out of the room as the tip of her tongue runs across her bottom lip. I feel a twitch in my pants. For a second I think she might walk over to me but the soft gaze quickly turns into a hardened expression as she places her phone on her desk and then flips me off.

"She wants me." I grin as I slap Teller on the shoulder and walk back to my office.

I'd be lying if I didn't say that I got joy out of coming up with ways to torture Kate. But hey, in my defense, I'm tortured by her presence. Those mile-high heels she wears make her tits bounce with every step and I swear to God she purposely presses them against me when she's close to me. She may act like she wants to rip my head off, but I'd bet my millions it would be after she fucked the life out of me.

I'm halfway through a contract when I hear her signature sharp knock on my door at the same time she turns the handle and waltzes in.

"Still haven't mastered the art of knocking, waiting for a response, then entering the room or walking away after three or two years, huh?"

She ignores my comment and my smile as she places two files on my desk. Only, she doesn't turn and walk out like usual; she stands stoically in front of my desk, hands clasped in front of her.

"Mr. Wells, I need a minute of your time, please." She's way too subdued; something's up.

"What can I do for you, Miss Flowers?" I see her flinch when I phrase it that way, which I do because she always gives me a reaction.

"I need to leave early today, around fourish, so I can go pick up my car."

"*Fourish?*" I repeat. "What time is that exactly?" I can see her tighten her fingers together; she's trying not to bite my head off.

"Four. I need to leave at four. The towing yard closes at five and it's outside the city."

"And why can't you do it tomorrow or Friday? You are off work on those days, right?" I lean back in my chair, my fingers steepled in front of me as she squirms.

"Well, yes, I am, but I had plans—"

"Yes, and it looks like *your* plans were interrupted because *your* car broke down. Those aren't my problems or the company's problems so take care of them on *your* time."

Her eye's twitching and I'm biting the inside of my cheek to keep from laughing. It's not that I'm an actual maniacal asshole; it's just that this is a game we always play. She purposely makes mistakes or shows up late just to piss me off and make me look incompetent and I make her life difficult in return. We both get a free pass for telling each other off and don't go running to HR to solve our disagreements. I contemplate giving her a lecture on being a responsible adult but feel I've pushed her buttons enough for the day.

"Will there be anything else, Miss Flowers?" I say in my sweetest voice.

"No, sir." She says the words through gritted teeth before marching out and slamming my office door.

"Well, look who it is, Miss Fifty Shades of Brown." I'm surprised to find Kate sitting at the bar at my local watering hole by the office. After her mere meltdown at work today, I figured she'd be tending to her car. She slowly turns her gaze toward me. "Whoa, don't go spitting green vomit all over me," I say, raising my hands in the air.

"Shouldn't you be sneaking into people's houses right now, stealing presents and destroying the happiness of innocent young children?" She leers at me.

"What the hell is that supposed to mean?" I wave to flag down the bartender. "I'll take a vodka soda. Belvedere, please."

"Please tell me you get that it was a reference to *The Grinch*? It's the holidays; you'd think that you'd be a little nicer this time of year like the rest of humanity but my guess is your heart hasn't grown three sizes yet." She motions to the bartender for another round for herself.

"It's the holidays? Hadn't noticed." I shrug. It's a lie, I noticed, but I don't like to celebrate them. They're not as fun and jolly when you're alone.

"Yeah, what gave it away? The lights, trees, holiday music, and general merriment?"

"Man, you're extra snarky today. You get a fresh batch of bitch hormones or something? Must be something about you redheads." I shake my head and thank the bartender as he hands me my drink. I go to take a sip but I'm startled when Kate slams her hands down on the bar, making me jump and spill my drink a little.

"My God, can't you just let some things slide? Why do you always have to be a massive prick all the damn time?"

"You don't make it easy, sweetheart." I wink at her and I know she fucking hates when I flirt with her. I'm sure as far as she's concerned it's just me trying to piss her off but the reality is, it's genuine. There's something about her copper hair and bright-blue eyes with those overly full pouty lips. I catch myself lingering a little too long on her lips as she glares at my remark. "Okay, fine. I'm sorry. I'll be nicer. But only if you tell me why on God's green earth you're wearing that outfit." I can't hold back my laughter any longer.

"You told me to see if anyone had an extra outfit because I wasn't allowed to go home, and the only person who had extra clothes was Marge." She downs her second cocktail and motions for another.

"Marge!" I laugh even harder. "Well, for what it's worth, you wear Marge's clothes much better than she does." She doesn't respond, just smiles as the bartender hands her another cocktail.

"Hey, could we each get a double shot of tequila?" she asks him and he nods.

"Whoa, what's up?" I ask as she dives into the drink.

"Like I said, the holidays."

"Shitty for you too, huh?" She shrugs but I'm curious so I pry. "Tell me about what's going on."

"Seriously? Are you just going to make fun of me the entire time?"

"Nope," I say, raising my right hand. "Hand to God." She stares back at her glass for a moment before letting out an audible exhale. The bartender is back and places the double shot down in front of us.

"I'm gonna need this first," she says, grabbing the shot. She doesn't wait for me, just takes the shot and sucks on the lime it came with. "Shit!" she says, slapping her hand down on the bar before coughing.

"You're a natural."

"Anyway, I took tomorrow and Friday off to drive home to my family's house. They live a few hours away, in central Illinois, but now, since my car broke down and it got towed, I have no way to get home. So thank you!" she says, reaching over and grabbing the second shot right from my hand and downing it.

"What the hell? What do you mean thanks to me?"

"My car wouldn't start at the bakery so I had to leave it and of course it was a fifteen-minute parking spot so I went back at lunch, it had already been towed and you wouldn't let me leave work early to pick it up. I called a few mechanics and because it's the holidays, nobody had a spot open for me, except one place but they had to have my car by tonight. Soooo, I'm shit outta luck. But the funny thing is, I don't even have the money to get it fixed anyway." The liquor is starting to hit her. I can see her eyes are a little blurry and her movements are a little delayed and exaggerated as she speaks.

"Shit," I murmur and I really do feel like dick. "Kate, I'm so—"

"Kate?" she says loudly. "Kate? I thought I was Miss Flowers." She barks out her own name, clearly trying to do an impression of me. I can't help but laugh which in turn makes her laugh.

We spend the next hour laughing and drinking, something I never thought I'd be doing with her. It feels nice, great actually.

"So are you close to your family?"

"Meh." She shrugs. "I mean yes I am but there was an *incident* that kind of changed things." She leans forward and whispers the last part, resting her hand on my thigh. I instantly flex against her warm touch. I'd give anything to have her keep going. She glances down, though, almost as soon as it happens and looks at her hand and then back up at me, her eyes dropping down to my lips. The moment feels charged, sexy even, but then she jerks her hand back.

"Tell me," I say.

"My ex, Chad. He's going to be there."

"Well, first off, that's the problem right there… Chad? That's a frat boy douchebag name. Chad, Derek, Kyle—they'll break your heart and leave you with an STD." She snorts. "Wait, your ex will be at your family Christmas?" I wrinkle my nose at the thought.

"Yeah, we dated for three years and my family loved him. They had every right to; he's great, really he is. He just ended things kind of abruptly last year right before Christmas and yeah, my family still loves him."

"That's fucked up, Kate. You know that, right? Do they know it bothers you?"

She waves her hand sloppily at me. "It's fine. I'm not gonna make a big deal out of it. Should be fun to meet his new girlfriend."

"He's bringing his new girlfriend?" I know I sound like a gossipy middle schooler but who the hell does that to their daughter?

"Yeah. I think he might have cheated on me with her 'cause they were always *just friends*." She uses dramatic air quotes while rolling her eyes. "Whatever, it's fine." She waves me off again but I'm seething. I know I have no right; she's not mine and our relationship is a dumpster fire most of the time, but there's still a protective feeling I have toward her.

"Okay, here's what's going to happen. I'm going to drive you home."

"What?" She tumbles forward off her stool and I catch her.

"I'm taking you home to your family's Christmas. Like you said, it's my fault you don't have a way to get there now so I'm going to fix this."

"No, I can't let you—" I hold my finger up to hush her lips; they're soft and pillowy and I regret it as soon as our skin touches.

But instead of pulling away, I run my finger along her lip before pushing her hair behind her ear. Her big eyes are fixated on mine. I grip the tip of her chin with my thumb and pointer finger and pull her just a tad closer.

"I'm taking you home and that's final, Miss Flowers."

2

KATE

I wake to the sound of loud pounding.

"What the hell happened?" I can't figure out if the pounding is in my head or coming from the front door. I lift my head off my pillow and my stomach rolls. I look down my body and see that I'm still in Marge's outfit and there's an awful taste in my mouth. I groan and drop my head back on my pillow just as the banging sounds again.

"Kate! Open the door, Kate!" The voice is muffled but I can still distinctly make out who it is.

Confused, I climb out of bed and stumble through my bedroom and toward the front door. I pull it open, greeted by an overly chipper Damon Wells.

"What are you doing here? How—how do you even know where I live?" He looks me up and down and laughs before pushing past me inside.

"I'm guessing you don't remember anything about last night?"

"Oh God, what happened last night?" My hands shoot up to cover my face and my stomach rolls again.

"You okay?" he asks as he steps around me, toward my kitchen. He grabs a glass off the counter and fills it with water before handing it to me.

I take it from him, eyeing him suspiciously as I drink it. The coolness instantly helps to calm my stomach. I need something for this pounding headache.

"Sit, I'll make you some toast so you can take Advil. Got any juice?" he asks as he shrugs out of his coat and places it on the back of one of my barstools.

"Again, while I appreciate all this," I say, making a circling hand gesture, "what are you doing here?"

"You *really* don't remember anything about last night?" he asks again through a laugh as he pours me some orange juice and hands it to me. "I found you at Franklin Tap after work; you were already a few cocktails deep and after some pleasantries exchanged between us, you started ordering double shots of tequila. But not before you explained everything about your car to me and that because of me you had no way home to spend Christmas with your family so I said I was taking you home and you agreed."

I spit the orange juice out of my mouth which simultaneously comes out my nose in the process. I grab a paper towel and bury my face in it, trying to minimize my embarrassment.

"You're what? No, no. Absolutely not!" I say as I take the toast from him and take a bite. I continue to shake my head as I swallow it down.

Damon leans back against the counter across from me, crossing his arms over his chest as I continue eating. I stare at him, his silence and direct eye contact making me uncomfortable. *Dammit, why does he look so sexy standing there like that?*

"Are you going to say anything?" I finally ask, overwhelmed by my discomfort.

He doesn't say a word, just hands me three Advil. I take them and finish the rest of my toast as he reaches forward and takes the plate from me. He places it in the sink and then slowly walks over to me. He spins the barstool around so that I'm facing him and then reaches down, grabbing my hand and pulling me to my feet. He wordlessly leads me down the hallway and into the bathroom.

"This is weird; what are you doing?" I ask as he reaches his arm into my shower and turns the water on.

"Your parents' house is just over three hours away. We have about twenty minutes to get on the road before we're behind schedule. So get in the shower while I pack you a bag."

I point a finger in his face. "You are not packing my bag! Creep, you'll probably touch all my underwear or something." I narrow my eyes on him as he takes a step toward me and I take a step back. My back hits the countertop and I reach my hands out behind me to brace myself.

"Am I going to have to help you undress too?" He cocks his head to one side as his eyes lazily roam up my body.

What the fuck? I instinctively throw my arms over my chest to cover myself as if this giant turtleneck isn't already doing that for me.

"Get out!" I bark at him as I point toward the door. Once he exits, I let out the breath I didn't even know I was holding and lean against the door. A smile involuntarily spreads across my face and my lower belly tightens when I think about the look that was on his face as he looked me up and down. The way my body responded was a surprise too, the tingling between my thighs.

"Oh God. Ew! Nope," I say to myself before clamping my hand over my mouth and shaking my head back and forth. I will not be another woman to fall prey to Damon Wells and his manwhore ways. *Gross!*

I pull my shirt over my head and slide Marge's skirt down my thighs. I finish getting undressed before stepping into the shower and scrubbing myself from head to toe. It's only now I realize that I never showered after being covered in coffee, Chicago street slush, and train germs.

After I shower and feel somewhat human again, I crack open the bathroom door and look around to make sure Damon isn't creeping on me before darting across the hall into my bedroom. I pull a pair of oversized jeans on and one of my favorite holiday sweaters, a cat wearing a Santa hat that says 'Meowy Christmas.'

"Did you borrow that from Marge too?" Damon asks, eyeing me over the lip of his coffee cup.

"Did you make coffee?" I ignore his comment and walk over to the fresh pot of coffee on the counter.

"Here, poured you a cup already. Has milk, a splash of creamer, and a Splenda in it already."

I eye him suspiciously as I bring the cup to my lips, hesitating before I take a sip. "You poison this? How do you know how I take my coffee?"

"We've worked together for over three years now, Kate; I know how you take your coffee." He lets out a little snort and just shakes his head like I'm being ridiculous.

"And in those three years you've never once made me a cup of coffee."

"No, that's *your* job," he says, pointing a finger at my chest. There it is, the elitist attitude I've come to know and hate from him.

"So anyway, about driving me home. While I truly appreciate the offer, it's just unrealistic. Are you going to drive me there, then come all the way back here, then come pick me up again? That's like twelve hours of driving over a few days and that's without holiday traffic and Illinois snow. Plus, I cannot take you away from your family and holiday plans. And most importantly, I don't want to spend the holidays with you. I'm afraid that you'll suck all the joy out and get us permanently blacklisted from Santa's *nice* list." I tack on the last part just to remind him that spending time with him is about as much fun as getting a pelvic exam.

"Come on, let's go," he says, completely ignoring everything I just said and taking my only half-drunk cup of coffee right from my lips.

"Hey, I'm drinking that!" I say as I lunge for it but he blocks me with his forearm.

"We'll get more on the way." He rinses both our cups out and then marches over to the front door, pulling it open. "Kate," he barks loudly and gestures for me to walk out the door.

"Are you hearing me right now? What the hell is your problem, Damon? I told you I'm not going and I don't even have a bag or anything ready." I place my hands on my hips and dig my heels into the ground.

"I told you I would pack your bag and I did; it's already in the car with your purse and I have your keys. So I'm not going to tell you again." He dangles the keys in front of me, his voice lowering with his last statement. I don't respond; I just stand there with my biggest *fuck you* expression on my face.

Before I can register what's happening, Damon takes two large strides toward me and picks me up, tossing me over his shoulder before spinning around and marching through the door.

"Put me down, you psychopath!" I scream as I beat against his back. It doesn't faze him; he slams the door and locks it before heading down the stairs. He tightens his grips around my waist and I feel his bicep flex against me. I've never seen Damon out of clothes, but damn does he feel built. His imposing six-foot-three frame lends to his dominant demeanor but knowing he's rock-solid as well... My thoughts come to a screeching halt when I remember what's actually happening right now.

"This is kidnapping! Help! I'm being kidnapped!" I wail as he kicks open the door to my building and marches us out onto the sidewalk.

"Nobody cares, sweetheart," he says, smacking my ass and causing me to yelp in response.

He slides my body down the front of his, placing me unsteadily on the ground. He reaches around me, opening the passenger door to his Tesla X. I widen my stance, ready to refuse getting in when he forcefully hooks his hand behind my neck and pulls me to within mere inches of his face.

"Of course you drive a Tesla," I mutter.

"Don't create more of a scene, Miss Flowers. Just get in the fucking car or I'll make a scene of my own and trust me, it will put yours to shame." A shudder runs down my spine at his almost whispered words.

"I'm not easily bullied, Mr. Wells," I retort confidently. "In fact, I think you're all talk." I mirror his whispered tone back to him as I defiantly push a finger into his chest with a cocky smirk. I barely make contact with it, though, before he grabs my hand and pulls it over my head while backing me up against the car. He pins my arm above me as he tightens his grip on the back of my neck, pulling my face to his until his lips are on mine.

I'm confused as to what is happening as the distance between our bodies disappears and I can feel him pressed firmly against me. He tips my head slightly as his lips begin to move against mine. It's only soft for a second before he delves his tongue into my mouth. He swirls it around mine once, twice, then pulls mine into his mouth and sucks on it. The sensation shoots straight to my core and I immediately want more. But before I can reciprocate, he's broken the kiss.

"Jesus, why the fuck do you insist on making everything so damn difficult?" He pants. He releases my hand and neck and spins me around to put me in the passenger seat. This time I don't fight him. I'm dizzy and confused and extremely turned on. He pulls the seat belt over me and then leans in a little further to threaten me once again.

"Next time you insist on defying me and making a scene, I promise you, the punishment won't be so nice." He slams the door and walks around to his side and climbs in.

I don't know what the hell just happened but I know for damn sure that any momentary laps in judgment I've had over the years where I've wondered, if even for a brief second, what Damon Wells would be like in bed, I just got my answer and I can guarantee I won't be forgetting it anytime soon.

3

DAMON

Why the hell did I have to kiss her?
    I know why I did it. I've wanted to kiss her smart, sexy mouth since about fifteen minutes into our first interview. You'd think a woman that calls me an arrogant prick wouldn't get the job but that's when I knew I had to hire her. I didn't want a kiss-ass or a pushover; I wanted someone who would be my right hand and call me on my shit. That's exactly what Kate is. I trust her more than anyone and I know she has zero reason to ever lie to me to keep her job.

I'm sure I'm a clinical head case, and I probably have all sorts of shit I need to work through in therapy. But the only way I've been able to put a dividing line between us is to be as unappealing to her as possible. I'm not an idiot; I see the way she looks at me when she thinks I'm not looking. It's the way most women look at me. The problem isn't that I don't still drool over her as well; it's that I don't want to be the guy that breaks her heart. So I maintain my arrogant, heartless prick ways around her so that even if she finds me attractive, she'd rather deal with disposing of my dead body than waking up next to me.

"There's a Pilot about thirty minutes outside the city that I always stop at. Obviously you don't need gas but they have the best road trip snacks and there's a Starbucks across the street." She doesn't look at me when she talks, instead staring out the passenger window. I'm actually surprised she didn't fly into me and rip my head off once I got in the car. Maybe she's still in shock.

"Sounds good to me."

We drive the rest of the way to the Pilot station in silence. I follow her around the giant gas station as she grabs a few snacks. I step away and grab some water for us before meeting her at the counter and handing my credit card to the cashier.

"I can pay for my own stuff."

"I'm aware, but I can pay for it as well." I want to offer her a smile when I respond but there's zero amusement on her face as she grabs her things and rolls her eyes. We pretty much repeat the same process in the Starbucks drive-through. Only this time she lunges across my seat with her app open, trying to get the cashier to scan hers instead of mine. I win.

"What was with the *of course you drive a Tesla* comment earlier? What's wrong with a Tesla?" I ask as she takes a drink of her coffee.

"Nothing, it's a fine car." Her answer is clipped.

"So basically anything that I do is going to piss you off?"

"How would you feel right now if your boss showed up to your apartment and carried you kicking and screaming out of your place after going through your shit and then kidnapped you?" I can't hold back, and I burst out laughing at how dramatic she's being.

"I didn't kidnap you, Kate. You agreed that I would take you home for the holidays. The only reason you put up such a fight is because you can't stand me for some reason and you insist on always making everything difficult instead of putting aside your disdain for me so that you can at least enjoy the holidays with your family."

She doesn't respond right away, just sulks in silence while she continues drinking her coffee.

"It's not that I can't stand you," she finally says quietly. "You're just always so mean. It's like you can't ever let a single dig get by you."

"Might I remind you that you're the one who first started all this in our interview. You called me an arrogant prick, Kate. Not exactly starting off on the right foot."

"You laughed when I said it and you deserved it; you told me that I was indistinguishable from the fifty other candidates you had so why should you spend another second interviewing me."

"Yeah, and yet you still took the job." I give her my best smile and it actually makes her laugh a little.

"Thanks."

"For?" I raise an eyebrow and she lets out a dramatic sigh before answering.

"For taking me home. I know I didn't make it easy, but I would have been really sad missing out on it."

"You're welcome." I don't know why but I reach over and grab her hand for a moment, giving it a small squeeze.

"What are you going to do though? Will you make it back in time to celebrate with your family?"

I don't want to answer her question because I don't want to explain that I don't have a family to celebrate with.

"Uh, I'm staying with you and your family. I'm not doing four trips, Kate."

"No, that is not happening. I'm sure there's a hotel in the area."

"Are you going to make this as difficult as you did this morning or can we just get that all out of the way now?" I ask her sternly.

"What are you going to do, Damon? Throw me out of the car this time?"

"Remember when you were a kid and your mom would say, *'Don't make me pull this car over or you'll regret it?'*" I give her a wink and she rolls her eyes and crosses her arms over her chest with a huff.

"Don't you see how weird this is going to be? Spending Christmas with my boss at my own family home? What am I supposed to tell them?"

"Well, what did you tell your mom in the text you sent her last night?"

"What?" She bolts upright, her eyes about to bug out of her skull.

"You said you texted your mom when we were sitting there at the bar and she was super excited you were bringing someone." I can see the panic building on her face.

"I texted her?" she squeals as she frantically looks for her phone. She pulls it out of her purse and opens her messaging app. "Oh, gaaaaawd," she says, smacking her hand against her forehead.

"What did you say about me?" I ask as I try leaning over to look at her phone.

"Keep your eyes on the road!" she says, pointing ahead as she scrolls through the messages. "Well, it's not as bad as I thought. I just told her that my car broke down so a *friend* was bringing me home and that he'd be celebrating with us."

"Why did you just do air quotes when you said friend?" I ask.

"Because that's how I sent it to my mom; I put friend in quotation marks because you're my boss, not my friend. Please don't tell me this comes as a shock and your feelings are hurt?"

"No, I'm just trying to read it as your mom probably did and when you said a friend in quotes and then 'he' along with it, she thinks you're bringing home a lover." I wriggle my eyebrows up and down at her.

"A lover? Gross. Why'd you have to say it like that?" She wrinkles her nose at me.

"Fine, a boyfriend."

"No. She wouldn't just read into my texts and make something up like that. Besides she'd have asked me that in the text." She shakes her head matter-of-factly.

"What was her response to your text then?"

She stares at her phone for a minute before closing her eyes and pinching the bridge of her nose.

"Shit," she mutters.

"She said, and I quote, '*Ohhhhh, a friend? Tell him we're excited to have him celebrate with us. Let me know if I should make up one of the guest rooms?*'"

"And did you respond to that message?"

"Nope. I probably blacked out." She pulls her foot up into the seat and rests her arm on it as she stares out the window.

"What's our story going to be?" I finally ask after several minutes of silence.

"I guess just what I told her, that you're a friend and my car broke down and I needed a ride."

"You don't think they'll find it strange that this random friend that they've never heard of spends the holidays with you?" I'm not sure what I'm getting at here but I'd rather use the boyfriend angle with this whole thing.

"Not as weird as my boss bringing me home. Look, I don't tell my parents about every friend I have or guy I meet so it won't be weird. Just—" She trails off and I can hear the irritation in her voice. I don't want to upset her but I can see by her bouncing leg that either the caffeine has kicked in or the closer we get, the more anxious she gets.

"Want to talk about it?" I finally ask. She looks over at me suspiciously. "Chad. Yeah, you mentioned him too last night." She doesn't say anything right away. "We don't have to. I'm just offering a listening ear if you do want to vent."

"I love being with my family at Christmas but, yeah, having him there when he might have cheated on me and my family still loves him… It's not the best feeling."

"Can I ask why you didn't tell them?" I'm genuinely curious about this dynamic.

"I didn't have proof; it was just a gut feeling because she was always with him and he was cagey about their texts and when I would bring it up, it turned into a fight and she was always *just a friend*. Then, two months later, he was dating her and they were exclusive. Now they live together, eleven months after he dumped me." She shakes her head and lets out a pathetic laugh. "It wasn't worth it to cause a huge dramatic thing between him and me and my family. I know if he did cheat and I had proof and told my family, they'd believe me and back me up but—"

"Your family shouldn't need proof. If you feel hurt by their actions and betrayed, they should respect you."

"I know but it's more complicated than that. Like I said, I don't want to burn bridges or cause drama. I can put my feelings aside for the holidays," she says with a weak smile and it pulls at me. I want to punch this Chad guy in the face and his balls and tell her family to respect their fucking daughter. I grip the wheel a little tighter.

"You still love him?" I probably shouldn't ask it but what the hell; she seems to have let her guard down a little.

"No. That's part of why I don't make it into something with my family. I don't want to give him the satisfaction of even thinking that I'm still in love with him. I got over him as soon as he started dating Tess."

"Ugh, Tess. I know a Tess. There's something about that name," I say and it makes her laugh.

We spend the rest of the trip in silence. Kate nodded off about an hour before we arrived. I caught myself a few times glancing over at her. She looks so peaceful when she sleeps. Gone is the constant scowl and the claws are fully retracted.

"Kate." I reach over and shake her, the GPS indicating we are about fifteen minutes from her parents' house.

"Oh shit. I didn't realize I fell asleep. Did you pack my mak—?" I reach behind her seat and grab the bag of makeup and hair products that I packed for her.

"Thanks," she says as she unzips it and frantically pulls out random objects. Not even ten minutes later she's running her hands through her fluffed up hair and slicking a gloss on her lips that smells like peppermint. My dick twitches when I think about tasting that gloss right from her mouth.

Nope, keep those thoughts at bay, I remind myself, but then thoughts of taking her in her childhood bedroom has my blood pressure soaring. We're pulling into her parents' driveway and a little plan formulates in my head. This one might actually end up getting me murdered, or at least my dick ripped off, but fuck it.

"Damn." I whistle as we pull up the large driveway to the three-story brick mansion. "How did I not know your parents were rich?" I ask as we climb out of the SUV and I grab our bags.

"Because we're not friends and that's a weird thing to share with people. Okay, please, please, please be on your best behavior and don't flirt with my mom or push my buttons." Kate glances over her shoulder when she hears someone calling from the front porch.

"Sweetie, hiiii!"

"That's my mom," she says hurriedly. "Promise me, Damon!" she says, pointing a finger at me as I wave and smile at her parents that have now both gathered in the doorway.

"Don't worry, sweetheart," I say without moving my lips. "I'll behave." I carry our bags as we walk up to the front door and are immediately greeted by not only her parents but several other people.

"Hi, I'm Laurie Flowers, Kate's mom and this is her father, Dennis." They both shake my hand as Laurie points to another man and woman. "And this is our oldest, Oliver, and his wife Erin. They're expecting our first grandbaby." She claps as she says this and Erin shrugs and rubs her belly.

"Don't forget about me!" someone says in the back as they come walking out of the kitchen, a huge grin on the man's face.

"And this is Chad and Tess," Laurie says as Chad juts his hand out toward me. I shake his hand and have to stop myself from snapping it off. I plaster on my fakest smile.

"Chad, good to meet you. Heard *so* much about you," I say.

"Chad and Tess just stopped by briefly to give us some lovely holiday wine that his mother made. They got into town from Chicago yesterday. I told him he could have just brought it to the party but he insisted once he heard you were heading home tonight." Her mom is so oblivious it makes my head hurt.

I reach down and squeeze Kate's hand, but she quickly pulls it away.

"Mom, Dad, this is Damon, my—"

"Boyfriend," I say, reaching out and pulling Laurie in for a tight hug.

"God, I've been dying to meet you guys." I grab Dennis's hand and give it a hearty shake.

"We're so happy to meet you too," Laurie coos as she gives Kate a big smile. If there's one thing I know how to do, it's charm the ladies and Laurie is no exception.

I feel a hard pinch on my backside and look over at Kate who is bright red.

"I'm sorry we haven't come down sooner. We've just been so caught up in our tight love bubble; it's like the entire world ceased to exist," I say, wrapping my arm around Kate's shoulders and planting a big kiss on her cheek.

She laughs, her face softening into a big smile as she rests her hand on my chest and leans into me. She reciprocates my kiss by reaching up onto her tiptoes and kissing my cheek, wrapping her arm around my neck, and then she whispers in my ear.

"You better pray for a Christmas miracle, sweetheart; otherwise, this is your last one."

Yup, she's going to kill me.

4

KATE

I can feel my face burning red but what I can't tell is if it's embarrassment, desire, or anger. Part of me loves to feel his big, strong arm wrapped around me while his hand grips my waist. It's possessive and sexy—something I've never felt in my past relationships.

To Jason, my first boyfriend, I was more like a best friend who made out with him and occasionally gave him hand jobs in my parents' basement. Around his football buddies he'd act like I was just one of the guys.

To Brody, my college boyfriend, I was basically a wallet and a sex toy. We barely spent any time together outside his friend group and the only time he sweet-talked me was when he needed money or wanted to get laid.

But that's why I fell so hard for Chad; he was different. He was charming and sincere; he knew all the right things to say to make a girl swoon and send butterflies soaring through my stomach. He'd compliment my outfit or when I tried a new hairstyle. He never had a passcode on his phone and gave me the password to his computer and email to prove that I could trust him. That's why I felt so blindsided when things changed. It wasn't a gradual change either. We didn't grow apart or have some huge disagreement about where we see our lives going. One day, he just had a passcode on his phone and he changed his computer password. When I questioned him about it, he just blew me off and said he'd had a passcode on his phone for almost a year now. When I pressed further, he said it was because his company demanded he do it since he could access private client information from his phone. I knew at the time it was a lie but I excused it. I ignored the little butterflies that no longer were flutters of excitement but little nagging reminders that something wasn't right.

Month after month things began to change even more. He started working late, going to more work events and dinners that previously I'd accompanied him to but now he told me I'd be bored. He even started traveling for work suddenly, something that his job had never required of him previously. I saw a new name, Tessa, popping up on his phone rather frequently and when I'd question him, he'd say she was just a friend, a coworker, that she was going through a divorce, etc. Again, I knew it was all lies but he had such a way of pulling me into his arms, kissing me, telling me how much I meant to him and how much he loved me that I'd ignore the feelings and tell myself that I was paranoid. It also didn't help that he texted my family more than I did and had become almost inseparable with my own brother.

"Mom, we'd love to freshen up if the rooms are ready? Yesterday was a bit of a hectic day, and we had a rough start today. Right, babe?" I turn to look at Damon and give him a sickly sweet smile.

"Yeah, this sweet little lady's car broke down yesterday, ended up getting towed, and just set the entire day up for failure, but you know how she is." Damon pulls me in tighter to his side and it takes everything I have not to pinch him again. "She kept that radiant smile and positive outlook going like you wouldn't even know her world was falling apart."

"Oh, honey," my dad finally says, "why didn't you tell us you were having car trouble? I would have gladly called Niles and told him to run you over a new one." My dad's business partner, Niles, lives full-time in Chicago and he's constantly trying to get me to call Niles about living in one of his many vacant condos.

"It's fine, honestly. I called a garage and they're taking it in next week when I get back. Mom, the rooms?"

"Well," she says with a pause. "Your room has been made up and is all ready to go. I made sure to have fresh towels placed in your bathroom as well."

"So, just the one room?" I ask, trying to somehow wordlessly convey to my mom that I really need two different rooms for us.

"Yes, dear," she says with a coy smile. I let my shoulders drop, realizing that she thinks I'm making sure that we are sleeping in the same room.

"Great, thanks so much, Mom." I lean forward and give her a kiss on the cheek. "I'll show us to *our* room then," I say as I turn to face Damon.

"Hey, Damon, great to meet you, man," Chad says as he slaps Damon on the shoulder before turning to me. "And Kate, sweet Kate, so great to see you too." He pulls me in for a tight hug that lingers way too long. "Tess and I are heading out, but we'll see you at the annual Flowers Christmas bash!" He gives my dad finger guns and it makes me want to puke.

"Let's go," I mutter under my breath to Damon as we walk down the main foyer toward my bedroom.

The moment we walk into my bedroom I slam the door behind us, causing Damon to jump and spin around. "What the fuck, Damon? My boyfriend!" I yell.

"Wow, okay. You're welcome first of all, and second"—he makes a lowering motion with his hands—"keep your voice down; they'll hear you."

"You're welcome? What happened to the plan we agreed to stick to, Damon? That you're just my friend? What the hell were you thinking?"

"First of all, what good-looking single people are just friends to the point that they go to family holidays together? Hmm? That's suspicious. Second, it just kind of popped out of my mouth when I saw that dickweed *Chad* standing there with his toothy grin and ridiculous handshake." He mockingly thrust his hand out and distorts his voice. "Hi, I'm Chad, a cheating manwhore that's bamboozled all of you."

"Typical," I say as I grab my bag off the floor and toss it onto my bed.

"What's that supposed to mean?"

"It means that you are so arrogant and entitled that you don't listen to anyone else. You think you know better than everyone else even in their own lives. You managed to weasel your way into my family Christmas and then instead of doing what we agreed on, you go off the rails because you act on impulse and think you know better than me. I'm just so tired of it." I sit down on the bed and cradle my head in my hands. I want to cry I'm so frustrated and still tired from being hungover. Not only do I have to face Chad and Tessa all weekend, but I now have to put on a show and act like I'm dating my boss. I feel the bed move a little as Damon sits down beside me and puts his hand on my shoulder.

"I'm sorry, Kate. I really am. I just—truthfully, I felt sorry for you when I saw that Chad was there with the woman he cheated on you with and everyone was acting like it was okay. I just wanted to—I don't know, fix it for you?"

I know he probably thinks he means well but his apology just pisses me off even more. I shrug his hand off my shoulder and stand up.

"You feel sorry for me? God, Damon, I didn't ask for any of this from you. I don't need or want your pity. I can take care of myself and my feelings and handle my ex being here, okay? Let's just get one thing straight between us; you're my boss and not my boyfriend. We aren't friends; we don't even like each other. Let's just pretend, get this weekend over with, and go back to our normal dysfunctional working relationship." I rifle through my bag, pulling out my clothes and putting them into the dresser drawers. Damon doesn't move off the bed for several seconds. I can see something in his eyes, but I don't linger long enough to decipher what it is. I feel a twinge of regret for snapping at him so harshly again but instead of apologizing, I just remind myself of the dozens of times he's made me cry at work.

"Uh, can my stuff go in these drawers?" he asks, pointing to the second dresser. I nod and we both continue to organize our stuff in silence.

"Can I just ask... Why not let your parents help you? You

mentioned not having the money to fix your car at the bar last night so...?" His words trail off but I don't answer so he keeps talking. "I mean, clearly they're not hurting; this house has gotta be at least ten thousand square feet."

"I don't really feel like talking about it," I say as I gather my toiletries and head into the en suite. I close the door behind me, placing my things on the counter. I put my hands on the counter and stare at myself in the mirror. As much as I tried to make myself look alive with some makeup in the car, I can see the prominent bags under my eyes. My eyes look dull and sad; my hair is limp and lifeless. I turn on the shower and allow the room to fill with steam for a few moments as I strip out of my clothes.

When I step into the shower, I can't hold back the tears that have been threatening for the last forty-eight hours. It's cathartic but it doesn't do much to help relieve the constant stress I've been under for the last several months. My parents always told me that I could come home when I moved to Chicago after dropping out of college. It wasn't just out of the goodness of their hearts that they offered me a place to stay; it was because they never believed I could make it on my own, and as the days and weeks go by and my stress and anxiety builds, I'm starting to realize that maybe they were right.

5

DAMON

I feel guilty for upsetting Kate, but I feel like she's overreacting. I just wish she'd explain why she won't just tell her parents what Chad did. I understand not wanting to ruin Christmas, but what kind of family wouldn't support their child? Not to mention, at some point you have to stand up for yourself.

I finish putting away my clothes and pull out my phone to check a few emails. Since Kate is still in the bathroom, I take the opportunity to look around her room. From the looks of it, I'd say it hasn't been touched since she moved out. I walk over to the bulletin board on the wall. It's covered in pictures, a few playbills and concert tickets, and a deflated mylar birthday balloon that's tacked to the wall.

There are pictures of her with friends, her volleyball portraits, her at prom, and several that look like she's in a play or production of some sort. I lean in a little closer; the emotions on her face are so perfectly captured. Her eyes are almost half closed because she's smiling so big, her cheeks pink and full, and she's embracing another girl so tightly. Once again, I'm reminded that this is a side of Kate I've never seen, not once in three years of working together.

I know she's right about me—I'm a prick, entitled, and arrogant. I hate the way I am half the time, but each time I think I'm going to take the high road with her or respond in a way that might get a better response out of her, I end up going below the belt. Somewhere along the way I convinced myself that if she hates me, I won't fall in love with her, but I know that's not possible. I fell for her a long time ago and now I just do it to try and remind myself that I don't deserve her. I've always been terrified to let her in, to see the real me because if she doesn't hate me and I'm not making her life miserable, then there's no excuse if she doesn't want to be with me. It's fucked up, childish, and misogynist. I want to change—I have to. She deserves it.

The bathroom door opens and she walks out slowly, her wet hair stuck to her neck. She glances at me briefly before scurrying over to her closet and tossing her clothes in the hamper. She's wrapped in a fuzzy robe that goes to her ankles; her lack of makeup emphasizes the smattering of freckles across her nose and cheeks.

"You were in theater in school?" I ask, pointing to the photos.

"Yeah." She grabs her makeup and walks back in the bathroom.

"Hey, can I talk to you for a minute?" I ask, shoving my hands into my jeans. She hesitates but turns back and walks over to the bed to take a seat. "You're right. I had no right to make decisions for you and certainly don't have a right to fix anything for you. This is your life and I did weasel my way into it and I'm sorry." She doesn't say anything so I keep going. "This is your home and your bedroom and I'm clearly making you uncomfortable. I don't want to do that, Kate, especially during Christmas, so I'll tell your parents that I have an emergency back home that I need to take care of and let you guys celebrate in peace. I'll even send someone else to pick you up or leave my car here and take the train back to Chicago."

"No, no," she says, shaking her head. "That's too much, Damon. Weasel was probably too harsh of a word. I was angry and honestly the fact that you offered to bring me here and miss your own family Christmas is... extremely selfless and I haven't been as grateful and appreciative as I should be."

"Well, I can at least move to another guest room; this place has to have a few others or at least a couch I can crash on so you get your own space." I watch as she seems to contemplate the offer for a minute before shaking her head.

"No, this is fine. I feel like if you move to another room, it will just bring on more questions and draw more attention to our little sham of a situation." I nod in agreement. "But don't think for one minute you aren't sleeping on the floor," she says, grabbing her makeup again and heading for the bathroom.

"It's a king-sized bed. Come on."

"Not a chance in hell, buddy." She shuts the bathroom door in my face and then quickly re-opens it. "I'll be out of here in fifteen minutes. My parents eat dinner at six p.m. on the dot so there's plenty of time if you want to shower but don't go wandering around out there without me. I can't trust you to not say something else to make things even worse."

"Can I shower while you do your hair and makeup?" I ask, trying to look past her into the bathroom.

"Ew, no." She scrunches up her face like I just offered her a cockroach as a snack.

"Ew? Seriously?" I say, placing my hand above her on the doorframe and leaning in a little bit. "You didn't say ew when my tongue was down your throat." I smirk.

She gives me that snarky-ass look that makes my cock hard before slamming the door in my face. I laugh. Even if she doesn't want to admit it, she's attracted to me just as much as I am to her.

The door flies open again. "And don't be going through my room." She tries to shut the door again, but I put my hand up to block her. "What are you doing?"

"You're taking too damn long and it's already five forty. I'm taking a shower while you do whatever it is you're doing." I march past her and take in the large bathroom. There's a jacuzzi tub in the corner and large walk-in shower. "Want to put that to good use?" I point to the tub and she just rolls her eyes.

"Seriously, get out."

"Avert your eyes," I say as I pull my hoodie and t-shirt over my head. "Or don't. Up to you." I kick off my shoes and pull my socks off as she looks at me in horror. I reach for my belt and undo the buckle, her eyes slowly falling from mine down my chest to my waist. I see her swallow hard and I realize that she's turned on. I stop my movements and take two steps forward till I'm standing in front of her. I reach my hand up slowly and place my fingers beneath her chin.

"What do you want to happen next, Kate?" I whisper the words and I see her eyes searching mine. She wants to know what I want, but I won't give her the satisfaction. I want to hear the words from her lips; I want her to say that she wants me, that she needs me as badly as I need her. I step forward again. This time she's against the counter and my body is almost flush against hers. I reach my other hand up and I place one on either side of her face. "It's just us in here, Damon and Kate. Whatever happens can just be left here, in these moments." I lean in, my mouth a centimeter from feeling her sweet, pillowy lips again. "Do you want me, Kate?" I start to close the distance when there's a loud knock on the bedroom door and it's immediately opened.

"Kate, sweetie, dinner is al—oh! Oh goodness. I'm so sorry." Laurie blushes and pretends to cover her eyes as I take a step back.

"We'll be right down, Mom," she says as she waves her off.

"I see where you get the knocking as you open the door thing; it's a Flowers family trait," I say as she pushes me away and turns back to face the mirror. I want to resume what we were doing; it's killing me not knowing what she would have said or if she would have let me kiss her again. I don't dwell on it though. I unbutton my jeans and pull them down my legs along with my boxers, kicking them to the side before stepping toward the shower and flicking on the water.

"Jesus, Damon, what the hell?" Kate asks as she throws a hand up against her eyes.

"It's just an ass, Kate. Relax. Plus, the glass is frosted." I step into the shower. "You've seen a man's ass before, right?"

"Yeah, I look at your face every day, don't I?" she quips and I can tell she thinks it's a zinger. I burst out laughing at her corny joke. She always comes up with these little one-liners that she thinks are so clever and they always work because I always end up laughing.

Ten minutes later we're both dressed and walking down the stairs for dinner. I grab her hand right before we enter the dining room and at first she stiffens, but then I feel her fingers entwine with my own.

"So," Laurie, Kate's mom, begins, "how did you two meet?" I'm surprised it's taken them this long to ask, if I'm honest, considering two seconds ago they've never even heard about me. I glance over at Kate who has a nervous look on her face as she takes a sip of her wine.

"Through work actually. One of those classic both working for a big company and met in the elevator situations." I smile genuinely while I reach beneath the table and squeeze her hand. I'm not sure why but I don't want to lie to her family any more than I have. "I know for me it was love at first sight," I say, giving her a wink. She rolls her eyes at me and smacks my hand away.

"Speaking of work, Kate, whatever happened to that asshole boss you worked for?" Laurie asks as we begin to eat. Kate chokes on her wine and I reach over to pat her on the back as she grabs her napkin. I take the opportunity to ask another question because I can't wait to hear what her family has to say about me.

"Which guy is this?" I furrow my brow, trying to look convincing.

"*D* something?" her mom says as she's trying to remember his name. "His first name started with a *D*."

"Derek!" I say enthusiastically and they all agree.

"Yes, Derek," her brother chimes in. "He's a total prick apparently. Has one of those uppity frat guy attitudes and treats her like shit. I told her she should have sued him for harassment and then walked out with both fingers in the air."

I glance over at Kate and I see the blush creeping up her neck; she's mortified. She waves her hand dismissively as she takes a sip of water and clears her throat. "He's not that bad; you guys are blowing it out of proportion. Besides, it's Christmas. We don't want to talk about work."

"Not that bad? Sweetie, didn't he make you cry like every single day for the first several weeks? That's awful and honestly I wish you'd let your father speak to him."

Shit. Is that true? I made her cry? I knew I was harsh but she gave it back just as good so I thought… Fuck, I feel like an idiot.

"Apparently he's got a small you know what," her mother whispers as she points to her lap.

"Is that right?" I ask as I reach my hand under the table and rest it on Kate's thigh. She tries to push me away but I don't budge. "And how would you know that, baby?" I say in my most syrupy voice.

"I don't *know* that; it's just an assumption since it seems like his personality is so dickish, I can't imagine there's a lot in his pants." She reciprocates my cheesy smile. "Enough about my boss's penis, okay?"

"Damon, what is it that you do again?" her father, Dennis, asks me.

"Investment banking, sir. Not very exciting I'm afraid."

"That's an excellent career, son. One can never go wrong with finance. Got me where I am," he says, lifting his glass and gesturing around the massive dining room.

"Cheers to your success, sir; you're an inspiration, truly," I say as I raise my glass and everyone follows suit.

"And cheers to hoping that Derek's tiny penis gets chewed off by a rabid raccoon and he finally gets what he deserves," Laurie chimes in and I can't help but burst out laughing.

"Mom!" Kate says in utter shock.

I can't wait to tease her about this later.

6

KATE

"Your father and Oliver are going to play chess in the lounge, and Erin and I are going to pretend to watch them but just gossip and talk about our holiday party tomorrow night. Care to join us?" My mom loops her arm through Erin's elbow.

"In a bit, Mom, but I promised Damon I'd give him a tour of the house. Show off all the amazing Christmas decorations." I give her a smile and a kiss on the cheek as she follows my dad and Oliver down the hall toward the lounge.

Dinner was a shit show. The food was outstanding and the wine flowed a little too freely, but I owe Damon an apology or at least an explanation for what my family said about him.

We walk into the great room where my mom's signature fourteen-foot-tall spruce is immaculately decorated in shades of gold and silver with the perfect touches of red and green.

"This looks professionally done," Damon says as he walks around the tree.

"That's because it is." There's a garland decorated with a red velvet ribbon and twinkle lights throughout it wrapped around both of the banisters and the balcony of the landing. There are also two massive wreaths on either side of the tree, each above a mirror.

"Hey, I owe you an apology about dinner," I start as I walk over to where Damon stands admiring the tree.

"Nah, honestly they could have said a lot worse and they wouldn't have been wrong," he says, slipping his hands into his dark-gray dress pants. The motion causes them to tighten against his taut ass and images of his naked backside pop into my head. I shake my head as if it will make the thought disappear.

"I, uh—" I laugh and nervously cross and uncross my arms. "I know we haven't always been friendly or even nice to each other but, ugh, I don't even know what I'm saying." I'm flustered and he can see it; he gives me a warm smile before reaching out and tucking a strand of hair behind my ear again. Something about that movement is so simple yet intimate.

"Just say whatever you feel, Kate. I'll listen."

"I obviously complained about you a lot to my family, well, not a lot, but I told them a few stories. I know it hasn't been all you. I can be moody and difficult and instead of telling you when something is hurtful or rude, I snap back and clearly it never resolves anything." I stare back at him, wanting him to say something but also worried he'll ruin my attempt at an apology with a snarky-ass remark.

"I understand and I'm sorry I made you cry. I'm sorry for so much more too." He looks at me like he's sincere and I feel like I can see regret in his eyes.

"So what is this, like a clean slate or something?" I poke him in the side and he laughs, a deep rumble that fades into a smirk. There it is again, that tension between us. I don't want to ruin the moment so I turn to face one of the large mirrors and stare at my reflection.

"It's a shame it's all fake; we do make a damn good-looking couple." He sidles up behind me, placing one hand on my waist as the other pulls my hair off my shoulder. I watch in the mirror as his eyes follow his hand movements, settling on my neck for a moment before meeting my gaze in the mirror.

"Cut it out, lovebirds. Dad wants you to play him in a game of chess, Kate." Our moment is interrupted by Oliver walking around the tree. "Damon, I've got some single malt scotch with our name on it." He gestures with his hand for Damon to follow him. I give him a nervous shrug as I walk toward the lounge to find my dad.

"My parents always made me feel like I was going to fail when I dropped out of college and moved to Chicago," I say into the darkness of my bedroom.

"Why?" Damon asks from the floor.

After losing in chess to my dad, I decided to head up to bed a little early. Damon was still sipping scotch with Oliver while they played pool. I stopped by the game room to say good night but changed my mind at the last minute, instead just sending a text to Damon to let him know I'd retired for the evening.

I've been lying in bed for the past two hours, trying to fall asleep, but I can't. My mind won't let me. I've been trying to rationalize my feelings for Damon, not just the attraction but the genuine interest I've started to develop for him. It made me do a postmortem on my relationship with Chad and try to resolve if I should let it go or tell my parents how he hurt me. And now, the question that Damon asked me earlier about why I didn't ask my parents for help has been rolling around in my head.

"They wanted me to come back to my small town and work at my dad's company and find some guy to marry who would also work for my dad. I just didn't have that academic bug like Oliver did; he flew through school like it was nothing, getting his undergrad and two masters in the time it takes most of us to just figure out what we want to study." I stare up at the ceiling, Damon not saying anything else. I don't know what comes over me but I can't seem to stop talking.

"Every time I talked to them on the phone they'd tell me that my bedroom hadn't changed and I could always come home. I know it sounds like something normal parents should offer, but it wasn't because I said I was struggling or needed help; in fact, I was excited about my new life in the city. They weren't interested in hearing what I wanted to do, what was going on in my life—they just wanted me to move back home and take the safe route. So when I met Chad, who was a little older and established and rich, they were elated. They loved him and always said we were perfect together. They were just happy some guy was there to pick up the pieces of my messy life and pay for it. I think to them, Chad was my redemption so when I ended it with him, they took it personally as well. I think to them, I was once again throwing my life away because I was choosing happiness over security and that's just something my family cannot understand." A tear forms at the corner of my eye and I don't resist it; I let it fall. "I hate feeling sorry for myself." I sniff. "I know I come from wealth and privilege and I sound like I'm complaining that my gold shoes are too tight, but that's why I didn't ask them to help me with my car. I want to do it on my own. I want to pursue my dreams and be happy for me, even if that means I have to struggle."

The room is so silent, just the sound of my sniffles here and there. Damon doesn't say anything; instead, he just reaches his hand up on my bed until he finds mine. He holds it like he knows that I just need someone to listen and while it feels amazing to be heard, it causes my heart to ache because I know it's all an illusion and will disappear like a vapor once we return to work.

The next morning we sleep in, taking our time to get coffee and eat breakfast with my family. It's nearing four and my mom has officially moved into panic mode as guests for her annual Flowers family holiday party are about to start arriving. Damon and I managed to escape back up to my room to get ready and avoid most of the hysteria.

"You ready for this?" I ask as I brush some bronzer onto my cheeks.

"Yeah, I think so. How bad can it be?" Damon asks as he adds the finishing touches to his already perfectly styled hair. It was weird but Damon's hair was the first thing I noticed about him; it's thick, black, and so shiny. When he lets it grow a little longer, like it is now, his curls come through, sometimes casually falling over one eye. He looks over at me and I absentmindedly reach up and run my hand through the front to get the curl effect I like. He smiles at me and I smile back, the moment feeling so natural between us.

"So what did you and Oliver talk about last night? You guys were gone for like three hours." I try to sound casual but it's been eating at me since last night.

"Just typical guy stuff. Talked business, the markets, how he's getting ready for fatherhood." He steps out of the bathroom, returning a few moments later. "How does this look for a party?"

I almost choke as I give him a once-over. *Hot damn, he looks good!* He's wearing a black velvet suit coat with satin lapels over a crisp white shirt and a gold and black bow tie. His dress pants have a velvet tuxedo stripe down the side to match the coat.

"You just happened to pack the perfect black tie look for a holiday party?" I scoff. Like how does he seriously always look like he's ready to be served on a silver platter?

"Of course. I'm a man of style, baby; I always come prepared." He gives me a wink as he casually leans against the doorframe and adjusts one of his cuff links.

"Good thing I brought two dresses and one of them happens to be gold." I step around Damon and into my walk-in closet, closing the door behind me. I pull out the floor-length gold sequin dress. The sweetheart neckline accentuates my cleavage and shoulders while the thigh-high slit shows off the perfect sliver of leg. I adjust the dress, pulling on a pair of matching strappy heels. I do a soft glam makeup look, a touch of a brown smoky eye and a nude lip while my hair is in soft waves and pinned back on one side. I open the closet door, stepping out to see Damon waiting on my bed.

"You ready to go make Chad jealous?" I joke as I walk over to him.

"Gladly," he says as he stands up and circles around me. "I'll do whatever you tell me in that dress. Chad will be crying in the corner by the time I'm done."

"Easy, buddy; I was kidding," I say as I press my palm against his chest and playfully push him away as I make my way to the door.

The party was in full swing. I say hello to the many friends of my parents I haven't seen since last Christmas all while introducing Damon as my boyfriend.

"What is going on with you?" I whisper to Damon as his hands grip my waist.

"What? Nothing. We're supposed to be in love, remember?" he

whispers back as Chad and Tessa smile and wave at us. I plaster on my fakest smile and wave back.

"Eat shit," I say through my smile at Chad even though I know he can't hear me.

"You seem extra irritated, what happened?" I turn to face him. I can see the tension in his clenched jaw. "You were fine an hour ago."

"Him," he says, pointing toward Chad with his chin.

"What about him?" I ask, confused. Damon looks around before grabbing my hand and pulling me off to the side.

"Last night when I was talking to Oliver, he told me—" He rubs his eyebrows and I can tell he's clearly pissed off.

"Told you what?" My heart is thudding in my chest.

"He told me that Chad has spun this huge sob story behind your back about how he thinks you cheated on him. He apparently still loves you and said Tess is just a rebound. I don't know if he's told everyone in the family, but that's what he told Oliver, and I think your brother believes him."

It sounds like water is rushing though my ears, then it turns to ringing. "He—no, what?" I'm so confused and angry. I ball my hands into fists as I replay what Damon just told me. I spin around and take a step toward where Chad is standing before Damon grabs me by my shoulders and spins me back around.

"No, don't. I have a plan. You might not like it, but just trust me," he says before walking away.

I stand there, inhaling and exhaling deep breaths. I can hear the band finishing up their song, and then I hear a familiar voice through the microphone.

"Ladies and gentlemen, good evening. I know you don't know me. I've had the pleasure of meeting several of you, but for those I haven't, I'm Damon Wells, Kate's boyfriend. Kate? Can you come here, please?"

Confused, I walk into the great room where Damon is standing on the small stage. My legs are wobbly as I try to rationalize what the hell is going on and what Damon just told me about Chad. Everyone is staring at me and I try to muster a small smile.

"Baby, I feel like my life didn't begin until I met you. You are a force to be reckoned with—fiery, determined, and so amazing. You are the inspiration behind everything that I do and I cannot imagine a life without you. Katherine Renee Flowers," he says, stepping down and walking over to me. "Will you marry me?" He drops the microphone down to his side and tips my chin up toward his.

"Say yes," he whispers and I don't know what comes over me but I do.

"Yes," I say and it feels like all the sound has been sucked out of the room. Then I hear chanting.

"Kiss her! Kiss her!" And before I know it our lips are touching; his hand is in my hair and my arms wrap around his neck and we're kissing. It's sensual and intimate at the same time. I don't overthink it; instead, I just let myself fall. I feel his hand slide up the slit of my dress and grip my thigh as I moan into his mouth, and then I hear them chanting again, only this time it's filled with cheers and laughter.

"Get a rooooom!" someone yells.

I pull back and look at him; he's not smirking like I expected him to be. His eyes are hooded and lustful, hungry like he's about to devour me. Within a few moments the band is playing again and everyone's dancing. My family rushes over to congratulate us before my mom realizes that we need a moment to ourselves. I don't even register what anyone is saying to me; I'm just nodding and pretending to smile.

"Would you excuse me," I say just above a whisper before escaping to the hall. I take my shoes off and walk up the stairs to my bedroom, barely closing the door behind me when Damon walks in.

"Did I fuck up again?" he asks and I just bury my hands in my face and start to cry. He pulls me to him, wrapping his arms around me as I cry. We stay like that for several minutes before I sit on my bed.

"No, this whole thing is just fucked up."

"I was just pissed about what Chad said to Oliver. It made me see red when I saw him tonight and I just wanted to make him hurt like he hurt you." He takes a seat next to me and I turn to face him.

"You need to understand, Damon, this isn't a situation that you can fix. In fact, pretending to be my boyfriend and now my fiancé—" I laugh when I say the word because it's so ridiculous at this point. "It's only making things worse because at the end of the day, I now have to explain to my family why a second relationship has failed in my life. They're going to wonder what happened when I'm single next Christmas. I'm not mad at you; I went along with it at this point just as much as you have."

"I know I just wanted to make things be—"

"No, Damon. No." I reach over and grab his hand and squeeze it as he lifts his eyes to look at me. "I'm not yours to save." I stand up and walk to the bathroom to change and take a shower. Before I walk in, I turn back to him. He looks wounded and I know he doesn't want to hear it, but I have to say it anyway. "I don't need rescuing. I can take care of myself, Damon."

7

DAMON

I stare into the darkness of Kate's bedroom, her words bouncing around my head from earlier tonight.

"I'm not yours to save."

I want to save her, to protect her from all the harm in the world and the fuckboy assholes like Chad. I roll onto my side and pick up my phone. It is 1:14 a.m.

"Oh my God, if you light up your phone one more time," Kate groans and slams a pillow over her face. Seems like I'm not the only one who can't sleep.

"Maybe if I wasn't subjected to sleeping on this floor," I groan as I try to adjust myself.

"Your fault. You could have your own bed right now if you didn't say we were together and now stuck in the same room."

"Come on, let me in," I say as I stand up and nudge her leg. She pulls the pillow from her face and glares at me.

"No way!"

"That entire side of the bed is completely untouched; you don't even go near it." I gesture toward the opposite side of the bed where the covers and pillows are still undisturbed. She doesn't respond, just rolls over and ignores me.

"Fine," I say and lie back down on the floor. I wait patiently until I hear her breathing deepen, and then I sneak into her bed and close my eyes, falling asleep almost instantly.

I wake to sunlight streaming through the blinds. I stretch my arms overhead and glance to my right to see Kate's side of the bed is empty. I'm surprised I didn't wake up to a punch in the face or even worse, my dick. I swing my legs out from under the covers and sit up, looking at the clock to see it's almost ten thirty already.

"Kate?" I ask and see that the bathroom door is shut but I don't hear any sounds. She must have woken earlier and went downstairs already for breakfast. I stretch again and walk over to the bathroom, grabbing the door handle and opening it without hesitation.

What I don't expect to see is a butt-ass naked Kate fresh out of the shower. Her body is still dripping wet as her arms are stretched above her head, pulling her hair back from her face. I stand there in silence; it feels like time stands still as our eyes meet.

Holy fucking shit, she's hot. I suddenly forget how to swallow as I take in the long, lean lines that run down her body. *Are her boobs fake? They look too perfect.* I narrow my gaze, not seeing any scars.

"What the fuck, Damon!" Her screech pulls me back to reality as she lunges for the towel on the hook and covers her body.

"Sorry!" I lie as I slam the door shut. "I didn't hear you, I swear. I thought you went downstairs."

Fuuuuuuck. Now I have to try and keep my fucking brain in control every time I look at her. I cover my face with my hands. "I need a Christmas miracle," I mutter just as she whips the door open.

"Seriously? I wake up next to you and now you're walking in on me naked? Fucking creep," she mutters before walking into her closet and slamming the door.

"It's not like I was looking through a keyhole or something," I say back at her before walking into the bathroom to take a shower.

Kate has to finish up some Christmas shopping with her mom and sister-in-law, so I take the afternoon to head into town and get some work done. I find a local cafe and knock out a few hours of work before taking some time to walk through the small downtown.

I see a jewelry store and decide to pop in. I'm greeted by a sweet older lady with gray hair. "Hello, what brings you in today?"

"Just looking," I say. I smile back and walk over to a small Christmas tree that holds several crystal ornaments. I'm about to walk away when one catches my eye. It's a crystal rendition of Thalia and Melpomene with a beautiful red ribbon through the top. Without a second thought, I take it to the counter. They gift wrap it beautifully in a small gold box. I don't know if Kate is still as into theater as she was when she was in high school but the images of her on the stage and with her theater friends looked like such a wonderful and happy time in her life. If I can give her something that even reminds her for a second of that time in her life, it's worth it.

I walk back to my car just as three men in Santa suits and one in an elf costume come around the corner, laughing.

"Ho! Ho! Ho!" They laugh as they stumble down the sidewalk.

"Pub crawl!" another one shouts, handing me a flyer as they keep walking. I look at the sheet, noting a holiday-themed pub crawl tonight. I pull out my phone and call Kate.

"Hello?" she answers.

"Hey, what are you doing?" I ask.

"Just finished up shopping with my mom and heading back home. Why, what's up?"

"We have plans tonight?"

"Nooo," she says cautiously.

"We do now. I'm coming back to pick you up. We're grabbing dinner and then hitting a pub crawl."

"You've never done a pub crawl? Ever?" I ask her again.

"Like I said before, no. My college experience was brief." She shrugs as she takes a sip of her beer. I watch her lick the foam from her lip and images of her from this morning come rushing back.

"What?" she says with that attitude and I have to bite my cheek from saying something inappropriate.

"Nothing. It just seems crazy because you live here. Pub crawls are staple small-town events. Every holiday has one."

"And how would you know?"

"Believe it or not, I lived in a small town once. Wasn't actually born and raised in Chicago." I regret bringing up my childhood immediately when I see the look on her face. She wants to know more.

"Where'd you grow up?" she asks and I wave the bartender over.

"Two candy cane shots," I say over the loud music and she gives me a nod. I turn back to Kate who's still waiting on me to answer. "Iowa," I say before downing the rest of my beer and grabbing her hand before she can ask more questions.

"What are we doing?" she asks as I pull her off the stool and over to a group of people gathered around a table.

"I signed us up for beer pong. We're next." I lean near her ear so she can hear me and I smell her perfume. It's spicy and exotic with a touch of cinnamon. It makes my mouth water and I let my lips linger near her skin. I step a bit closer, my nose in her hair and my lips against her ear. "Hope you brought your A game," I say as I smack her on the ass before walking over to the bar to grab our shots.

"Here, a little pre-game courage," I tell her as she takes the shot from me and we down them.

"Oh God." She shudders as she wipes her mouth with the back of her hand.

"Yeah, not good," I agree.

"I don't know how to play beer pong," she says in my ear.

"Don't worry, we're on a team. Just try to shoot the ping-pong ball into one of their cups. If you do, they drink it. If they get one in your cup, you drink it." She nods and we step up to play. It's a fucking riot. I've never seen her so relaxed and carefree. She's laughing, high-fiving strangers, and even throwing her arms around me and hugging me at one point. She's in her fucking element and I just sit back and watch.

"Stop it," she says, looking over at me. I'm sitting on the edge of a stool, watching her kick the other team's ass. After my third shot, I let her take over. She's better at the game than I am. Plus, it allows me to just watch her.

"Stop what?" I say with a coy smirk as I take a sip of my beer.

"Stop looking at me like that." She focuses her attention on her shot and takes it, kicking her foot back in the process and sinking it. She cheers again and points to the other team as the guy chugs his beer.

"Like what?" I say when she looks back at me.

"You know what." She plants her hand on her hip and juts it out. I just shrug and act like I have no idea what she's talking about. She takes a few steps toward me, abandoning the game as her eyes lock on mine and I can see the alcohol has given her a false sense of bravado.

"Now that you've seen me naked, you look at me like you don't know how to handle me." I reach out, grabbing her wrist and pulling her until she's standing between my thighs while I sit on the stool. I reach up, slipping my hand behind her neck and grasping her firmly. I pull her forward so that her lips are centimeters from mine.

"Sweetheart, I know *exactly* how to handle you."

Her breath hitches in her throat and we both ignore the yelling behind us to come back to the table. Instead, I stand up slowly, not releasing my grip on her neck. I grab her waist and spin her around, walking her backward a little till she's flush against a pillar in the middle of the room. I lean down, my lips hovering over hers, teasing her. I press my rigid cock into her belly so she can feel what she does to me. I'm teasing her; I want her insatiable with desire for me. I want her so frenzied she'll rip my clothes off by the time I get her back to her house. She steps onto her tippy-toes and our lips just touch when someone trips and falls into us, spilling beer all over her.

"Oh shit, my bad," the guys says, laughing as he stumbles and falls over.

"You okay, man?" I ask as I reach down and help him up.

I turn my attention back to Kate. "You okay?" I ask as she gives me a nod. I look her up and down; there's a wet stain all over her jeans and white sweater.

"Come on, I'll call an Uber. Let's get you home and cleaned up."

8

KATE

"Sit," Damon says as he grabs my waist and hoists me onto the counter in my bathroom. He grabs a towel and begins to dab it against my sweater, trying to soak the beer out of it.

He's standing between my thighs as he presses the towel against my side with one hand while holding my waist with the other. The warmth of his fingers through my sweater is doing things to me. He's focused on the task at hand so I take a moment to look at him, really look at him. His usually clean-shaven face has two days of stubbly growth and I want to reach out and run my hand against it.

"You confuse me." I say the words before I can stop myself and I know it's because of the alcohol but I don't want to take them back.

"How so?" he asks, looking up at me through his long, dark lashes.

"Most of the time you look at me like you hate me. Like I infuriate you so bad you either want to fire me or punch me, I can't decide. And then sometimes..." I swallow down the words. Should I open this can of worms? We were so close to kissing again tonight and I could blame it on the alcohol but I know that's not the truth. I want it to happen again.

"And then sometimes?" He repeats my words back to me.

"Sometimes you look at me like you want to bend me over your desk." I feel myself redden as I say each word. He stops what he's doing for just a second before letting out a small chuckle.

"You're not wrong." He smirks as he stands up and tosses the towel into the hamper.

"So, which one was it tonight? At the bar. I saw the way you kept looking at me." He stands between my legs, resting a hand on either thigh as he looks at me.

"You answer my question and I'll answer yours," he says.

"What question?"

"What are you going to do about this whole thing with your family and Chad?"

I push his hands off my thighs and jump down from the counter. Of course he'd ruin the moment. "I don't want to talk about it," I say as I step out of the bathroom and into my closet, Damon following close behind me.

"Why not? Is it because you're not going to do anything again? Even though this shithead is telling your family blatant lies about you, you're just going to pretend like everything is okay?"

"Can you get out so I can undress? I need to shower." I say the words calmly without looking at him.

"No. Why do you keep running from this, Kate? Please, just tell me why you refuse to grow a backbone and stand up for yourself? You have no problem at work standing up to me, telling me when I've been an asshole."

I turn around to face him. I'm angry and frustrated but he's not wrong. I don't know why I can't just tell my family that their actions with Chad hurt me. "I don't know, Damon, okay? I don't know." I fling my arms. "There. Are you happy? I'm a pushover!"

"No, no, I'm not happy. I care about you, Kate." He steps toward me and grabs my hand, but I pull it away.

"You care about me? That's rich," I mock.

"What the fuck is that supposed to mean?" he snaps back.

"You didn't give a fuck about my car breaking down and me needing to leave work early. You didn't care that I was covered in coffee and slush when I showed up late to work. You didn't care I had to wear someone else's clothes that didn't even fit me. No. Instead, you made fun of me and mocked my situation." I point my finger at him as I step toward him.

"It's not like that, Kate; it's not because I don't care or didn't care." He's exasperated and turns and walks out of the closet.

"Then why, Damon? So now that the tables are turned and I'm putting you in the hot seat to answer questions, you walk away." I follow him as he marches back into the bathroom.

"All of the above," he says with his back to me.

"What does that mean?"

"It means"—he turns around and walks over to me—"tonight, I want to do all of the above to you. I want to fire you, to punish you, to bend you over this counter and fuck some sense into you." He grips the back of my neck again. "Tell me," he pleads. "Tell me why you won't tell your family about Chad."

I stare at him, his chest rising and falling with his rapid breaths, and it hits me. He thinks it's because I'm still in love with him. "I wasn't lying; I'm not in love with him," I say and my eyes search his for relief.

"Do you still want him?" he says, his eyes falling to my lips.

"No." And before I can get the words out, his lips are on mine and his fingers are tangled in my hair. His kiss is hungry and needy, his lips covering mine as his tongue explores mine. Thrusting, massaging against mine as I feel him grow hard against me.

"Stop," I say as I step away from him.

"You don't have to do this; there's nobody around to convince that we're a couple or in love. I'm not in love with Chad. I'm totally over him but it feels childish to throw a tantrum with my family and ask them to choose me over him. It makes me feel pathetic, like the fact that I have to even ask my family for this just makes me feel less than. Why can't they see that it hurts me? Why can't they understand that it's just fucking weird to still have your ex-boyfriend hanging around all the damn time." I wipe away at the tear that falls from my eye and tumbles down my cheek. "I know it's even more pathetic that I complain about it but yet do nothing about it. I guess I felt that in time, they'd naturally grow apart. Then when he showed up with her, it just snowballed and now they all get along and I feel like the asshole that comes in and breaks it all up because my feelings are hurt. I just want to get over it and not fucking care. I'm so tired of feeling like the outsider in my own damn family."

We stand in silence for several seconds before Damon walks to me again. This time he doesn't hesitate. He pulls me in to continue the kiss, lifting me onto the counter again.

"I'm not trying to convince anyone that we're a couple right now." He grabs my hand, bringing it down to his crotch to feel his cock ready to tear through the zipper of his jeans. "I'm doing this because I fucking want you."

9

DAMON

I rest my forehead against Kate's as I feel her squeeze my cock in her palm. I can see her heart beating in the small, fleshy dip at the base of her throat.

"I haven't stopped thinking about the way your lips taste, wanting to feel them against mine again." I lean in and kiss her softly. "Every time you run your smart mouth, I want to teach you a lesson you won't forget." I kiss her again. "Every time you look angry, frustrated, or stressed, I want to ravish your body so all you can focus on is the pleasure running through you." This time I don't stop kissing her.

I place a hand on either side of her face, angling her mouth so I can deepen the kiss. She moans against my lips as her hands unbutton my jeans and slowly lower my zipper. My heart feels like it's about to beat out of my chest in anticipation of feeling her fingers wrapped around me. She doesn't hesitate; she slips her hand beneath the waistband of my jeans and boxers, gripping my cock. She pumps it once, twice, and I break the kiss to let out a groan.

"Fuuuuuck." My head lulls back as she continues to pump her hand up and down my rigid length. How can something so simple feel better than any fuck I've experienced? I steady my eyes on hers as I lean forward, placing my hand on the mirror behind her as I tip her chin upward.

"You've had me so fucking worked up for days," I whisper against her lips before kissing her. I reach my hands down and grip the edge of her sweater. I don't want her to stop what she's doing but I need her naked now. "Put your arms up," I say and she complies. I lift the sweater over her head and look down at her nude lace bra, her perfect tits spilling over the top of it. I'm about to lean down and pull one of the cups down when I look at her. "You're not talking, Kate. What do you want?" She stares at me for a moment.

"Take your shirt off," she says, reaching forward and undoing the buttons of my shirt. She gets three undone before I impatiently pull it over my head. I watch her eyes as they scan my naked chest. A small smile spreads across her lips, and then she bites her bottom lip as she reaches her hands out and places them on my pecs. She doesn't say a word as she slowly explores every ridge and muscle of my torso. I watch her intently; she looks like she's studying me and it's the sexiest thing. I tell myself she's memorizing this moment between us. My cock jumps and it's painful in my jeans. I reach into my pants and adjust myself, wincing a little in the process.

"Take them off," she whispers, and I look at her to make sure. She nods and I slip the jeans and boxers down my legs, kicking them off along with my socks. I'm standing in front of her, fully nude, my cock bouncing with my movements. I reach for the button of her jeans, undoing it along with the zipper before hooking my thumbs in the belt loops.

"Lift," I say and she plants her hands on the countertop and lifts her ass so I can pull her jeans off. I toss them on the floor and she's left sitting there in nothing but her bra and panties. "Don't look at me like that," I say as I step between her thighs again and lean forward, planting a row of soft kisses on her neck.

"Like what?" Her words are breathy.

"What'd you say earlier? Like now that I'm naked you don't know what to do with me?" I move her hair away from her neck, dragging my tongue up it before nipping at her earlobe. I feel her knees press against either side of my hips. "Trying to get some relief?" I murmur.

"Yes, please." She pants as she grips my biceps, her nails digging into my flesh. I reach a hand between her thighs, running my thumb over her still-clothed pussy. "Ohhh." Her mouth falls open as I repeat the process, circling around her clit a few times. I take a step back and her eyes pop open. I reach down and grab the edge of her panties, pulling them to the side.

"Oh, sweetie, you are already soaked. Look at those pink lips glistening for me. I think I need a taste, baby." I look up at her and she's intoxicated with lust. "But first, I want to watch you get even more wet." She looks at me with confusion. "I want to watch you play with yourself. Can you do that for me?" I grip her chin softly again. "Can you make yourself come for me while I watch?" A blush quickly creeps up her neck. "There's nothing to be ashamed of, Kate. I want to sit on the edge of the tub and stroke my cock while I watch you get yourself off."

"O-okay," she says, still a little unsure.

"What's wrong? You never had a man tell you exactly what he wants?" She shakes her head no and I lean forward and kiss her again. "Just pretend I'm not here; let loose and fuck yourself like you want me to fuck you, okay?"

I step back and sit on the tub, fisting my cock as she slowly pulls her panties to the side and begins touching herself. "Mmmm. Fuck, baby, that is divine." I try to keep a slow pace but it's hard the moment she lets her inhibitions go. I can see the moment it happens—her eyes close, her head falls back against the mirror, and she pulls her feet up to plant them on the counter. It's the hottest thing I've ever seen. Her creamy thighs splayed open, she works two fingers in and out of her wet pussy. I can hear the sounds it makes through her moans; she's pulled the cup down on one of her breasts as she fondles her pert nipple.

"Ahh, I'm close," she whimpers as she thrusts her fingers in faster and deeper. Her toes curl and she squeezes her nipple hard as waves of pleasure roll through her. I don't let myself come; I don't want to till I'm inside her. Instead, I stand and walk over to her, her fingers still inside her as she opens her eyes and looks at me.

"Did that feel good?" I ask as I reach down and pull her fingers from her folds. She watches me intently as I bring them to my lips, slipping them into my mouth and licking every ounce of her juices off them. I feel my dick aching. "Fuck me, you taste like heaven," I mumble as I drop to my knees and rip her panties off.

"Oh God, Damon!" I don't give her a warning; I dive face-first into her pussy, lapping at her. I use my tongue and fingers to pleasure her, drawing another orgasm out as she comes against my tongue.

"You want to get fucked, Kate?" I ask as I pull her off the counter and she wraps her legs around me. "If you don't want me to fuck you until you can't walk, you better tell me now." I grip her firm ass in my hands; I know I'm going to leave a bruise but that only makes me grip her harder. "Tell me, baby," I murmur against her lips.

"Fuck me, Damon."

She doesn't even finish the sentence before I'm sliding myself inside her, inch by inch; she's so tight. She grips my shoulders, biting me before sliding her hand into my hair and pulling so hard it burns my scalp.

"I can't hold back; this is going to be hard," I say as I thrust once more, eliciting an animalistic groan from her lips. I slam her back against the wall, pumping into her deeply with long, slow strokes. I reach behind her, undoing her bra. "Take it off," I groan as I watch her full tits finally bounce free. I lock my lips around one nipple, sucking it in and biting down softly.

"Oh my God." She pants over and over. She pulls my hair back so that we're looking at each other and for a moment I feel like she wants to say something, like she feels that this is so much more than a hard fuck in her bathroom.

I spin her around, planting her ass back on the counter as I look down and watch my cock slide in and out of her. "You've got me so hard," I grunt, my cock slick with her desire. "I don't want to come yet." She's leaning back a little on the counter, her head banging against the mirror with every thrust. I feel frenzied, like I can't control what I want to look at or touch while I'm on the edge. "Grab your tits, baby; play with your tits for me," I say as I grip her hips and start to pound into her harder and faster. She moans every time I slam into her.

"Touch my clit," she says and I obey. I lick my thumb, rubbing her softly as I feel her tighten around me. "Yes, yes, yes!" she shouts as she comes.

The moans, watching her lose herself in her orgasm, watching her delicious body beneath me, all of it sends me over the edge and I pull out just as I spill myself onto her belly and tits. I've been turned out with no release for days and it shows in the load I just dumped onto her.

We're both panting as we come down from our high. I reach down and pull her upright again, kissing her. "I wanted to kiss you when I was coming," I say and it shocks me. It's such an intimate desire to want or express, especially with someone who pretty much hates you and works for you.

I pull back for a moment to stare at her. "Are you okay?" I ask and she nods. She pulls me back to her mouth, her tongue flicking against mine like she's fucking my mouth with her tongue—it's hot as hell. "You kiss me like that again and you'll be on your hands and knees getting railed to kingdom come," I say, making us both laugh. "See what you did?" I say, looking down at my dick that's already ready for round two.

"I, uh, I think I need a shower," she says, lowering herself off the counter while looking at the mess I left on her. I grab some toilet paper, wiping her off the best I can before reaching in and turning on the shower.

She looks a little uncomfortable, standing there naked in front of me after the excitement of the moment has worn off. I turn her to face the mirror, the top of her head beneath my chin. I wrap my arms around her. Her green eyes look brighter, like they're sparkling, and her pale skin is reddened from my beard and tongue. "I like seeing you marked from me," I murmur in her ear as I cup her breasts. She puts her hands over mine, offering me a small smile before slipping out of my arms and pulling me into the shower.

10

KATE

Contrary to what I expected, Damon doesn't attempt to seduce me again in the shower. Instead, he sees to me.

"Turn around," he says as he squirts a healthy dollop of shampoo into his hand and begins to lather it. I do as he says and close my eyes as his strong fingers begin to massage my scalp. I inhale the minty scent of the shampoo, letting my shoulders relax as Damon strategically presses his thumbs into the base of my neck and runs them slowly up the back of my skull.

"Mmm, that feels good," I say softly as he pulls my back against his front. I feel his manhood press against my ass, but he doesn't attempt to pursue anything further.

"Good," he murmurs against my ear as he kisses my shoulder. "You deserve it." He walks me beneath the shower stream, rinsing my hair of the shampoo before reaching for the conditioner. He looks at me questioningly and I nod.

"Just the bottom half," I say as he squirts it into his palm and runs it through my hair. "I let it sit while I wash my body," I say, reaching for my loofah.

"May I?" He takes the loofah from my hands and squirts the body wash onto it. He lathers it before pressing it gently to my body as he begins to wash me slowly, his eyes trained on my body like he's studying me.

For a brief second I'm tempted to cover myself, although I have no idea why after I just masturbated in front of him. My cheeks redden at the memory but he doesn't notice. I watch him; he looks completely lost in the task at hand like he's worshipping me and it makes my stomach flop. Suddenly I feel nervous, giddy about what's happening between us, but then I remind myself to not overthink it. It's simply a product of us pretending to be together and getting carried away with it, mixed with an overabundance of alcohol at the bar.

After the shower I dry off and apply my skin care routine as Damon does the same. Neither of speak as we brush our teeth, towels wrapped around our still-naked bodies. When I'm done I turn to walk into my closet and glance back at him.

"Get in your pajamas and go to bed," he says with a smile. "I'm going to finish up in here and check a few emails." I give him a nod and head to the closet.

As I slip beneath the covers, the coolness of the sheets is a welcome sensation on my warm skin. I see the glow of the bathroom light still on beneath the crack of the door and I wonder if Damon will join me soon. I'm still wondering when my eyelids grow heavy and within a few minutes, I'm fast asleep.

The next morning I yawn and stretch my arms overhead before glancing to the left of me. The bed is empty but even stranger, the bedspread is unbothered. I turn my head back to the corner of the room where Damon has been sleeping, and there he is, still fast asleep with his naked back to me.

I lie there for a moment, taken aback at the fact that he didn't sleep with me after our escapades last night. *Should I be offended? Was I just a one-night stand?* I'm tempted to crawl over to where he's lying and wrap myself around him, see if he's ready for round two. But then I stop myself. What if that's all this was? Just a one-time thing and this is his way of telling me? Before I can overthink it anymore or act on my impulse to wake him up and ask him, he stirs awake and I roll over to avoid an awkward conversation.

I hear some rustling and then the bedroom door open and shut softly. I peer over the blankets, but Damon isn't in the room. I let out a sigh, trying to tell myself not to worry about last night. *It was just a momentary lapse in judgment; he'll go back to being your dick-hole boss in no time and you'll both hate each other again.*

"Don't fall for it," I say to myself in a hushed whisper just as the handle to the door twists and I roll back over. I hear the soft padding of feet on the hardwood floor, then the pressure of the blankets moving as Damon sits on the bed beside me.

"Good morning," he says softly as the smell of coffee hits my nose. I roll over and holy shit, I can't help but smile when I see what greets me. Damon, shirtless, mussed hair, and stubble lining his angular jaw, his sparkling blue eyes staring down at me. *Goddammit, there goes that little belly flip again.*

"Morning. Thank you," I say, sitting up and taking the cup of coffee from him. I bring it to my lips and inhale the sweet, creamy goodness before taking a long sip.

"I just spoke to your mom briefly and she said something about the annual Flowers family ice-skating event tonight?" He smiles and it feels like fifteen butterflies awaken inside my belly.

"Yeah, that's the tradition, I'm afraid. How are you on the ice?"

"I don't want to brag but let's just say my teacher told me I was a natural and gold medal contender." He gives me that signature cocking wink.

"*You* took ice-skating lessons? For how long?" I want to laugh when I picture him in tight stretchy pants and a blouse covered in a shiny sequins and bright feathers.

"From six to ten. Shhh, don't tell anyone or you're fired." He holds his finger to his mouth as if he's hushing himself.

"Scout's honor," I say as I lift my hand in the Girl Scout symbol. "Well, we usually have lunch as a family, go skating, and then hit up the Christkindle market in the town square for hot cocoa and pretzels. What time is it now?" I ask, reaching over and checking the time on my phone.

"Looks like we've got some time to kill," he says when we see it's only going on nine. "I have an idea." He reaches out and grabs my hand. "How about you show me around town? I want to see where Kate Flowers grew up and raised hell."

"You did not!" Damon says as he throws his head back and lets out a loud belly-aching laugh.

"I swear to God!" I say, his laugh making me laugh in return.

"So how long before they found it was you who put it on the marquee?"

We stand outside The Times, our local theater that has since shut down. The new cinema is located in the mall and this relic has been turned into a historical landmark. I'm telling him about the time I caught my best friend Grace's high school boyfriend Mark making out with Cherish, the head cheerleader, so I took revenge on him. He happened to work at the movie theater so I borrowed my dad's ladder. Grace borrowed her dad's truck and we snuck out and changed the marquee to read: *Coming soon, Mark Teeter's teeny peen starring in Cheaters are Douchebags.*

"Not long. Mark obviously knew Grace was involved since he worked at the theater and she had access to the letters when she'd come visit and he'd sneak her into the back to make out and fool around. She didn't tell him she knew about Cherish so the last time she visited him she stole the box of letters and the rest is history."

"You guys get in trouble?"

"Not too much. We both had to apologize to Mark and his parents but after we told Mark that we'd tell his parents and everyone at school that he was a cheater, he told us it was water under the bridge."

We stand face-to-face on the sidewalk. Our laughter has died down and Damon is staring at me. Normally it would piss me off or make me uneasy that he's staring at me, his body so close to mine, but this time it makes me warm and fuzzy. It feels like he can read my thoughts with only his eyes. I'm about to do something stupid like grab him and kiss him when the buzzing in my pocket snaps me back to reality.

"My mom just texted. Ready for lunch?"

"Very," he says, reaching down and lacing his fingers through mine as we walk toward Murdoch's Bistro after spending the morning walking around my hometown. Damon was insistent I show him my high school, the theater where my plays took place, and all my favorite hot spots. Of course, I have to remind myself for the four hundredth time that this all means nothing, and it's just an act. He's making the best of being my fake boyfriend—fiancé I guess—now, but once we're back in the office, the mask will fall away and we'll be right back to being oil and water.

Lunch goes well. It's easy and casual, and several times I catch myself smiling and telling stories and sharing laughter with Damon and my family like this is reality. I slip to the restroom after lunch. I'm washing my hands when I stare at my reflection. I look—*happy*. Panic grips me when I realize that I'm letting myself fall. Fall for the lies that we're both telling, fall for the fake romance that's brewing between us. I shake the thoughts from my head and step out, running smack into Damon's chest.

"Sorry—" I say, stepping backward without looking up to see who it is. In an instant he's grabbing my hand, pulling me toward him and kissing me like his life depends on it. I'm so shocked, I almost push him away, but I don't. Instead, I lose myself in the kiss, his hands cupping my cheeks, then one gripping the back of my neck as the other travels down my body, gripping my ass through my jeans and hiking my leg up around his hip. *Holy shit, this is hot.*

"Never be sorry," he says breathlessly as he pulls away for a second, peppering my lips with nips and kisses as I feel his hardened cock pressing into my center. I want to pull him into the restroom and rip his clothes off, acting out a repeat of last night. He kisses me one more time, deep and heated, his tongue swirling around my mouth as he releases his grip from my ass and places his hand on the wall beside my head. I'm about to ask what the hell that was about when I glance past his hand and see Chad staring right us.

"Look who joined us," he says without looking over at him and my heart sinks. That's what this was about, marking his pretend territory. I want to push him away, to slap him and tell him to leave and stop playing with my emotions, but I don't. It's not his fault I agreed to go along with this sham.

"Lovely," I say with a faint smile as I release my hands from his chest. "Can't avoid him forever." I push past him and walk back toward my family.

11

DAMON

I see the look on her face and I know she thinks I'm only doing this for show, but I'm not. I mean, yeah, I want that douche Chad to be jealous; I want him to see what he lost when he fucked up with Kate, but I also want her to see what's been right here in front of her this entire time.

I watch as she walks back to her family, a smile plastered on her face as she hugs Chad, and it makes my stomach sick. I know it's not my job to fix her life or make her happy. Hell, I guess it's insanity for me to even think that she'd look at me and see anything other than a grade-A asshole who's done nothing short of terrorize her for the last three years. Can I change that? Would it even do any good to tell her that what I'm feeling for her is very real, that all the past behavior was my way of simply projecting? I realize how fucked up it all is when I think it through. What kind of woman would want a man that was so insecure and scared he made her feel like shit just so he could feel better about not having her. I slam my hand against the wall, shake off the frustration, and make my way back to the table. I'll just have to do everything I can to prove to Kate that I'm more than just her asshole boss and apologize to her for what I've put her through. She has to see that I'm worth a second chance.

"Hold my hand," I say as we step onto the ice and Kate's baby deer legs slip beneath her.

"I swear I do this every year." She laughs as she grabs my coat with both fists and clings to me for dear life.

"I'll just tell myself you're pretending you need my help to boost my ego." I maneuver us so that her arm is looped through mine and her hand is in mine.

"Pretty sure your ego doesn't need any more boosting." She grips my arm but her attention is pulled away when she notices Chad laughing hysterically. I look over, following her gaze to see him and Oliver doubled over. My stomach instantly sours but I shake my head of the thoughts and try to draw Kate's attention back to us.

"What's your favorite Christmas tradition?" I ask. She looks at me and then gazes off into the distance like she's thinking about the question.

"Probably just being home with my family. I don't see them enough."

"You ever consider moving back here?" I ask and I'm praying her answer is no.

"No, not a chance. I am still very much in the need to spread my wings and fly and find out who I am phase." She giggles a little.

"That sounds corny but I just mean I still haven't figured out my career and I know that if I come back here, as much as I love my family, they'll guilt me into working at my dad's company because it's safe and predictable."

I unhook her arm from mine. "What are you doing?" she asks as I pull her till she's facing me.

"You trust me?" I smile.

"Absolutely not."

I grab her hands and begin to skate backward and she follows, a smile spreading across her face.

"Oh God, this is what my dad used to do with me when I was a kid and couldn't skate." She laughs and I spin her around slowly. She lets go of my hands and takes off. I chase after her and catch up to her just as she loses her balance and tumbles to the ground, taking me along with her. We lay in a pile on the ground, laughing.

"Are you okay?" I ask as I reach forward and brush her hair out of her face. She licks her lips, her eyes settling on mine as she nods her head. She's stopped laughing and so have I. Every time I look into her eyes my pulse races, my heart feels like it's about to beat out of my chest, and my stomach clenches with excitement.

"Kate," I say just above a whisper as I lean forward and catch her lips with mine. It's barely a kiss, a hint of a kiss as our lips brush.

"I think I'm ready to call it a night," she says, getting to her feet. "If it's okay, you mind passing on the Christkindle market?"

"Of course." I take her hand and lead us back off the ice where we turn in our skates and make the walk back to my SUV. I want to ask her what's wrong but I already know the answer. The moment the air thickened between us and our lips touched, reality came crashing back to her and she looked at me like I was just Damon Wells, her boss.

The car ride is quick but silent. So is the walk back to her room.

"You want to drink cocoa by the outdoor fire pit? It's only just after nine." I agree and we make our way down to the kitchen. I step onto the deck and turn on the fire while Kate makes us each a mug of cocoa before joining me outside.

"So Miss Flowers."

"Oh, back to Miss Flowers, huh?" She gives me a coy smile.

"Kate. What would be your dream job?" She lets her head fall back against the high back of the Adirondack chair, the steam from the hot chocolate in her mug rising and then disappearing.

"I still don't know but—" She hesitates briefly. "Don't laugh but I'd love to do something with theater or acting still. I just love everything about it."

"I think that's great; I'd never laugh at that." I furrow my brows a little at the thought that she thinks I'd make fun of her dreams.

"Well, it's not exactly corporate America, kicking ass and taking names like you, my dad, and my brother. Besides, you've never really been the type to encourage me to follow my dreams, more like 'get my damn coffee and so help me God if you spill it on my laptop again, I will ruin you.'" She says the last part in a mocking tone, like she's impersonating me.

"Man, your boss sounds like a prick," I joke, then take a sip of my cocoa.

"So was finance always your dream? What does your dad do?"

I feel my chest tighten the minute she starts asking about my family. "Yeah, I was always good with numbers and I knew I didn't want to do general accounting or just mathematics. I enjoy business as well so it worked out well for me. My dad is in construction. He didn't go to college which is why he insisted I go. Still made a good life for himself though, supported us," I say, hoping my answer suffices.

"Is it just you or you have any siblings?" she asks with genuine curiosity.

"This could seriously use some whipped cream," I say with a smile. "Have any?"

"I'm sure we do. Let me check." She gets up and walks inside, returning momentarily with a can of Reddi-wip.

"Hey, not to change the subject, but..." No, please do, I think to myself and feel a bit of relief at her comment. "I always hang out with three friends from high school when I'm home. It's our chance to catch up since they still live here. You're more than welcome to come but I also don't want it to be boring or awkward for you to hang out with more strangers."

I'm about to ask her if she wants me to come but I don't want hear *no* if she doesn't want me there. "I'd love to come; it's not a problem at all for your fiancé." I grin but she doesn't seem enthused.

"Well, I'm done." She tilts her mug to show me it's empty. "I think I'm going to head up to bed." I want to tell her to stay but I also want to follow her upstairs. Instead, I sit frozen, completely unsure how to handle this or what to do.

"Kate?" I say and she turns to look at me.

"Yeah?"

"I'm sorry." It's vague at best and I fully expect her to ask *what for*, but her face tells me she knows. "For—everything."

"Good night," she says and then stops in her tracks. I think she's going to ask me to join her but instead she turns and says, "And, Damon, it's okay, you don't have to pretend to be fiancé with my friends. They won't tell my family anything."

I give her a tight-lipped nod and it feels like someone just stuck a knife in my heart. "Good night, Kate." I smile as she walks away.

12

KATE

I brush the curls out of my hair; it falls in loose waves, tumbling over my shoulders and down my back. I slept alone again last night, Damon on the floor. I tossed and turned, debating on asking him to join me, but somewhere between my decision to talk myself out of it or say fuck it and jump him, I fell asleep.

Something is changing between us. The way he looks at me, the small, intimate touches between the overt, over-the-top kisses, send me spiraling down rabbit holes of what-ifs and maybes. But I always talk myself out of letting it be anything other than a fantasy. It's like when you go away to summer camp and you swear the guy you met is the love of your life and you're going to be best friends with the girls in your cabin forever, but then you go home and back to your real world and real life and it all fades away to just a memory.

"You look beautiful." Damon's voice interrupts my thoughts as I slick a plum-colored gloss over my lips. I turn to see him leaning against the door of the bathroom.

"Thanks." I smile. "You don't look too bad yourself." I let my gaze fall down the length of his body—he looks like a Christmas fantasy. Dark jeans hug his muscular thighs; the sleeves of his flannel shirt in shades of red and green are rolled to his elbows, exposing his forearms.

This man knows exactly how to dress to emphasize his long legs, lean waist, and broad shoulders. *Chris Evans who?*

"So anything I should know before being thrown to the wolves tonight? Or maybe something I shouldn't mention?" He runs his hand along his jaw seductively as his eyes roam over my body. I see him pause on my ass in the reflection of the mirror.

"Just be on your best behavior." I give myself one last look in the mirror as I walk toward the door, my hips swishing a little more provocatively than normal. I decided to wear the skintight black jeans Damon packed me, complete with a dark-purple off-the-shoulder sweater that not only shows off my neck and collarbones, but my cleavage as well. I didn't have the best shoes for the outfit but thankfully, my mom still had a pair of sexy thigh-high boots stashed in the back of her closet—I made a mental note to never ask myself what she wore them to.

"Always," he says before adding, "especially when people don't know me. First impressions and all that." I pause as I walk by him and rest my hand on his chest, flashing him the same seductive, coy smirk he loves to give me.

"Oh, they already know about you, Damon Wells. Trust me... They've heard alllll about you." And that look of *oh shit* on his face is exactly what I was going for.

WE CLIMB INTO THE BACK OF OUR UBER FOR THE SHORT RIDE TO the bar. It's quiet, the soft sound of Christmas jazz playing on the driver's radio. The pungent smell of a cinnamon air freshener fills the car.

It's a compact car, and our shoulders touch. But it isn't because there is not enough room but because Damon chose to sit in the middle of the back seat. He leans closer to me, his mouth close to my neck.

"So how worried should I be meeting your friends? They going to surround me in the alley and jump me?" he teases.

I can smell his cologne, notes of amber and pepper, and it instantly transports me back to the night in my bathroom. I feel warmth spread through my body at the memory that I've had sex with my boss. I know it sounds ridiculous to forget something so momentous from just two days ago but it's like I've compartmentalized it, convinced myself it didn't happen.

"Don't worry. After they took care of my first boss, they promised they wouldn't do anything like that again. People were asking too many questions, Feds got involved," I tease him back, waving my hand dismissively before flashing him a grin. "If Chad's still alive, then you've got nothing to worry about."

We thank the driver and exit the car in front of The Rowdy Farmer, the same bar my friends and I have been coming to for years. Someone exits and I can hear Mariah Carey crooning "All I want for Christmas" over the speakers.

"The Rowdy Farmer?" Damon asks, pointing to the large gold letters set against painted black brick.

"Hey, it's small-town Illinois; what do you expect? The *corny* names are part of the charm. Corny," I repeat, wiggling my eyebrows up and down to which Damon laughs and just shakes his head. We step inside and I glance around, spotting my friends in a corner high top table.

"Over there," I say, pointing toward Todd who is waving us over. As we approach the table, my friends jump up, greeting me with hugs and air kisses. I start to remove my coat when I feel Damon's hands helping me.

"Allow me," he says, sliding the coat down my arms and placing it on my chair. All three of my friends have the same expression on their faces, one I'm not looking forward to dealing with.

"Damn, girl!" Todd says, whistling and pointing to my outfit. "You clearly came here to break hearts and necks dressed like that."

I flick my hair over my shoulder dramatically and jut my hip out like I'm posing. "That's the only thing I know how to do." I laugh. I turn to Damon who has that look in his eyes again, the one that either says I want to punish you or I want to drag you to the back of this bar and have my way with you. I ignore it, turning back to my friends.

"Damon, this is Todd, Charity, and Bridgette," I say, pointing to each friend. They all smile and say hi, Todd giving him a handshake that lingers a little too long.

"This is Damon, my boss." Something flashes across his face, a look I know all too well—annoyance. I want to remind him that he could have stayed home if he didn't want to come tonight. I just hope it doesn't develop into one of his sour moods that ruins the night.

I reach to pull out my chair but Damon has it first, placing his hand at the small of my back as I take a seat. He pulls his chair right next to mine, taking a seat. Our arms are touching and I catch my friends noticing.

"So, Damon," Charity asks, "what brings you down to our little corner of the world from the big city?" It's a legitimate question and I know my friends were surprised to hear that my boss was traveling home with me. I didn't give them any more detail than that and I only told them because he said he wanted to come out with us tonight.

I glance over at Damon, trying not to show the nervousness I feel in my belly. Once again, he reaches under the table for my hand.

"Long story short, Kate was having car trouble and I was a selfish dick that didn't let her leave work in time to get it fixed so I brought her home." He looks at me, a crooked smile forming at one corner of his mouth as he slowly strokes his finger across the back of my hand. It sends a shiver down my back.

"Oh my God, that is so sweet of you." Bridgette rests her hand over her chest as she speaks.

"Wait, so are you spending the holidays at the Flowers'? What about your family?" Todd's confusion mirrors everyone else's and this time I'm the one that squeezes Damon's hand. I've picked up on the fact that there's something about his family that he either doesn't want to talk about or isn't ready to talk about.

"Yup, staying with us. His family is completely understanding," I say, brushing off the question. "How is it that we've been in this bar for five minutes and nobody has ordered a round of nog shots?" My question successfully changes the subject.

"Nog shots?" Damon raises an eyebrow.

"Yeah, it's one part eggnog and one part whatever liquor you want. Todd likes Goldschläger because it's cinnamon; Bridge, you drink peppermint schnapps, right? And Charity and I drink it with Crown because we're not crazy and trying to black out."

"That sounds interesting." Damon laughs. "I'll do one with Crown."

"I'll get the first round." I stand to head to the bar when Damon pushes back his chair and joins me. He places his hand at the small of my back again as we walk toward the bar.

I say hi to Deb, the bartender who's been here since I turned twenty-one, and place the order for the shots along with two rum and cokes for Damon and me. I feel his hands on my waist as he stands behind me so I turn to face him. He doesn't let go; instead, he pulls me closer before reaching up and smoothing my hair away from my face.

I'm confused. I want to ask him what's going on, but I also don't want to ruin the moment. I give him a small smile.

"Why are you nervous?" His normally bright eyes seem darker, hooded.

"Nervous? I'm not nervous." I feel my shoulders shrug dramatically like I'm trying too hard to play it cool. Without thinking I glance over my shoulder and realize that all three of my friends are staring right at us, mouths hanging open. *Shit.* I step back a little from his embrace.

Damon follows my gaze. "Ah," he says, releasing me and placing his hands on the bar. "Right, sorry about that." He hands his credit card to Deb and grabs the tray with our drinks. "Keep the tab open," he says as we make our way back to the table.

I feel... bad, like I'm hiding him. But we aren't together; we aren't actually a couple. We're lying to my family about us. Hell, we're lying to ourselves as well.

We spend the next two hours laughing till my stomach hurts, reminiscing about our childhood and catching up on what's been going on in our lives. Maybe it's the alcohol or maybe I'm caught up in the fantasy, but at times it feels like Damon and I are a real couple. I feel his hand rest on my thigh under the table. He casually drapes his arm around my chair at one point. He even wipes a drop of liquor from my lips with his thumb and then licks it off his finger.

"I need to use the restroom," he says, sliding off his chair and walking away from the table.

"Okay, what the actual fuck was thaaaaat?" Todd gasps as he slaps the table with both hands, causing me to jump. He grabs the small bar menu off the table and begins to dramatically fan himself.

"Yeah, Kate. I just about melted over here with that thumb-licking situation," Bridge joins in.

I wave off their comments. "It's just the alcohol, I'm sure." I take a long sip of my ice water because they weren't wrong, that thumb-licking thing was hotter than hell and if we were alone, I probably would be in the bathroom with him right now.

"Seriously, Kate, he's into you," Charity adds. I scrunch up my nose and shake my head.

"Okay, I want to believe you're just being coy and you're not that oblivious to the fact that he's super into you." Todd grabs my hands. "Sweetie, it's clear you both like each other. What gives?"

For some reason, again probably the alcohol, tears prick my eyes and my chin quivers.

"Ohh, honey, we didn't mean to upset you," Bridge says.

"No, you didn't. It's not that." I grab a napkin and dab at the corners of my eyes, making sure Damon isn't walking back yet. "You guys know he and I have a very rocky relationship at work. Well, things have been... different lately between us."

"Different how?"

"We have had some actual nice conversations and we—" I trail off, not sure if I should divulge this information. But Todd catches on.

"Oh my God, you guys hooked up?" He covers his mouth with his hands and I squeeze my eyes shut and shake my head.

"Tell us everything! How was it?" Charity and Bridgette both talk over each other.

"It was—amazing! Like, best I've ever had. He—" I hesitate again and then lower my voice. "He made me get off in front of him so he could watch while he jerked off, and then we had sex all over my bathroom!"

Todd pretends to fall out of his chair like he's fainting.

"He *made* you?" Charity asks, her eyes wide.

I nod. "He's not just bossy at work apparently. But I'm not delusional; I know that as soon as we're back in Chicago and at work, things will go back to how they were." I glance up to see Damon walking toward me, and the water I'm chugging makes me cough.

"So, yeah, Chad is still hanging around so that's been a treat," I say, changing the subject.

"Ugh, what a tool." Charity shakes her head, and Todd and Bridgette agree.

"What do you think about that whole Chad situation?" Todd asks Damon as he sits back down. I had really hoped we wouldn't talk about Chad tonight but in my panic I mentioned him.

"I think he's a waste of space," Damon says, finishing off his drink. "If given the chance, I'd be more than happy to teach him a few lessons." His eyes darken.

"But I also think we should respect Kate's wishes about it. Maybe letting him see her move on with someone else and be happy and fulfilled for once will be the best revenge." His eyes don't move from mine and my breath catches in my throat. I glance over at my friends and they're all staring at me with an *I told you so* look on their faces.

Damon turns his head, looking over at the dance floor where two other couples have begun to dance. A slow country song I'm unfamiliar with comes on the jukebox and Damon holds his hand out to me.

"Dance with me," he says.

I place my water on the table and slowly extend my hand to his, and he leads me onto the dance floor. He pulls me in close, his hard body pressed firmly against mine as he grips my waist. My heart feels like it's about to fall into my ass and my back is as stiff as a board.

"Relax," he whispers in my ear as our bodies begin to sway with the music.

I let out an audible breath, willing myself to relax in his arms as we move around the floor. I want to ask him what he's thinking, what he's feeling, what we're doing. He must see it all over my face.

"Kate, look at me." He tips my chin up and our eyes meet. "Stop overthinking everything; just feel the moment." He leans in, planting a soft kiss to my lips before continuing the dance. The song ends, but another quickly comes on. Damon doesn't let go of me or stop dancing.

I let my hand rest against his chest; the feeling of his body against my fingers is doing things to me. I look up at him again. This time I initiate the kiss.

"Can I take you home?" Damon murmurs against my mouth, and I nod my head yes.

"Do you understand what I'm asking you, Kate?"

He pulls back, his eyes staring into mine as his lips are so close, I feel his warm breath as he speaks. I bite my bottom lip, not wanting to assume, but I don't have to for long.

"I'm asking if I can take you back to your room"—he slips his hand behind my neck—"and strip off your clothes so that you're completely naked and at my mercy." He nips my bottom lip and a jolt of electricity shoots right to the junction between my thighs, wetness pooling.

"I want to explore every delicious inch of your body with my tongue," he whispers in my ear as his tongue snakes out and curls around my earlobe. My eyes roll back in my head and I've completely forgotten I'm in the middle of a dance floor with my friends staring at me.

"And then," he continues, dragging his lips up my neck, planting small kisses along the way, "I want to fuck you so thoroughly, so deep that no other man will ever come close to making you come like I will over and over again."

13

DAMON

I don't remember us walking off the dance floor or saying goodbye to Kate's friends. Hell, I don't even remember the ten-minute ride back to her house. But the moment we step inside her room, my brain is only focused on one thing—her.

I'm worried her guard will be back up, that she'll have talked herself out of it, but when I close the door and turn around, she's already on me. Pulling my coat down my arms, she thrusts her tongue in my mouth. I free my arms, reaching between us to undo the buttons of her coat as I remove it, letting it fall to the floor. I grab her hands, spinning her around and pinning her to the door. I break the kiss, both of our chests heaving.

"I'm in control tonight, Kate. Understand me?" She nods slowly and I kiss her again.

"There's so many things I want to do to you. So many things I've fantasized about over the years." I know I'm exposing myself to her, telling her that this isn't something that's new to me. No, this is a fantasy I've revisited dozens of times over the years.

I release her hands, pulling her toward the bed. I take my time removing her clothes, slowly removing her boots first before stripping her out of her jeans and top. She's standing there in her lace bra and G-string; her full tits look positively edible. My mouth waters as I take her in. "So fucking sexy. I don't know where to start," I murmur as I run my hand over my mouth like I'm actually drooling.

I sit on the edge of the bed as I continue to stare at her, kicking off my boots and socks and removing my shirt. I slide off the bed onto my knees. "Think I'll start here," I say as I run my nose up the center of her panties. "Been dreaming about eating your pussy all night."

She threads her fingers through my hair as my hands grip her hips. I plant a soft kiss through her panties before hooking my thumbs in them and pulling them down her thighs. I see a small wet spot inside her panties and smile. "Were you wanting me to taste you too?" I ask, looking up at her, and she nods.

I lean forward again, slipping my tongue between her folds, causing her to jerk and pull my hair. She hisses and I do it again. "Not like this," I say. Her eyes pop open and she looks down in confusion. I stand up, removing my jeans so my cock springs free.

"Get on the bed on all fours." She looks at me, then slowly moves to the bed, bending over and looking over her shoulder at me. "Fuuuuck me, that's a pretty sight." I look at her exposed to me, her glistening pussy and plump cheeks staring back at me, begging to be taken. I step forward and grab her hips, pulling her back till her feet are hanging over the edge of the bed, then I drop to my knees. I don't waste time. I dive in, lapping at her as I grip her hips, burying my face in her wet folds. Eating her from the back has been running through my mind since the second day I met her. She squirms against me, fisting the sheets and moaning as her release builds. I don't stop. I lick long, slow laps from her slit, all the way up her ass crack, swirling my tongue around the tight bud of her ass. I feel her jerk in surprise.

"You want more, baby?"

"Yes," she says, and I dive back in. I fuck her with my tongue, then I slide two fingers deep inside her as I continue licking her ass. It only takes a second before she's exploding around me, my name tumbling from her lips as she collapses on the bed. The sound of my name being groaned by her while she orgasms is about the best thing I've ever heard. I grip myself, stroking a few times, but I stop, afraid I'll come too early just by looking at her.

She looks at me, my cock in my hand. Her eyes drop to a small bead of pre-cum leaking from my tip and she pulls herself up, crawling over and licking it. My cock jumps at the warmth of her tongue.

"Fuck, baby," I say as she does it again and again, just the tip of her tongue swirling around the head of my shaft. She opens her mouth wider and I guide myself into her, sliding in and out of her lips a few times. It's a vision I'll never be able to unsee, Kate on her hands and knees, my cock fucking her mouth. I pull back before I can finish, a look of disappointment settling on her face. "Don't worry, sweetheart, we're just getting started."

I didn't bother bringing condoms on this trip—I wasn't exactly expecting this to happen—but Kate assures me she's on birth control and we're both clean.

I stand her up, reaching behind her to remove her bra. I cup her breasts, rubbing my thumbs over her nipples.

"That feels so good; I'm so sensitive," she says as her head lulls back. I lower my head, taking my time with each breast, biting and sucking on her nipples as I caress them. Her moans are driving me wild and I know I can't take much more.

I lift my head. "I need to fuck you so bad," I say as I kiss her. I walk us back to the bed and climb up her body, kissing her everywhere. I'm tempted to stop at her pussy again, her scent almost pulling me in. I lick her twice, savoring the sweetness before grabbing two pillows and placing them beneath her ass. She's at an angle now, her back and shoulders on the bed, her hips and ass elevated. I position myself at her entrance, teasing her a few times by running the tip up and down her slit.

"More," she pants, and I oblige. I thrust in an inch, pulling back out and thrusting in two. She's so tight around me. My eyes roll back in my head as she grips me like a vise. It only takes a few minutes before I've built up a rhythm, driving all the way into her and pulling all the way back out. We're both on edge, groaning, grunting, trying not come and just ride this out for as long as possible.

I lift myself up so that I grip the top of her headboard; her arms are outstretched over her head, palms flat against the headboard as I drive into her.

"I can't stop," I pant as I drive into her harder and harder. "I need to come, baby," I grunt as my pace begins to grow sloppy and jagged. I can't stop. I groan, slamming into her fully one last time until I spill myself inside her just as her release breaks free. She digs her nails into my back as she lifts her hips higher and grinds them against me. We're both breathless, falling into a pile of sweaty limbs.

"Nobody's ever done that before," Kate says, breaking the silence.

"Done what?" I asked, confused.

"Umm—licked my ass," she says softly, and I turn my head to look at her.

"Seriously?" I'm surprised in all honesty.

"Yeah, that's pretty wild for me."

"Hey." She looks up at me. "No need to be embarrassed by it. We're both consenting adults and as long as you enjoyed it, that's all that matters."

"I did enjoy it." She tries to bite at her lip to keep from smiling.

"Oh, yeah? Interested in any other new things?" I prop myself up on my elbow to look at her.

"Like?" She looks scared.

"Well, I'm not asking to fuck your ass; if you've never done anything like that, I don't think it's best to jump into that." She covers her face and giggles.

"Oh my God." I pull her hands down and even in the darkness of the room I can see she's blushing. "Not with that dick. I'll be ripped in half." I can't help but laugh; her eyes are huge and she's completely serious, but I've never heard it put quite like that.

"You ever had anything inside you? A finger? Toy?" I ask and I feel my dick start to stir at the thought of it.

She shakes her head no.

"Interested? If you're not, I won't push it."

She thinks about it for a second. "Maybe?"

She doesn't have to tell me twice. I reach down between us, my fingers finding her pussy and I begin to slowly circle her clit.

"We'll go slow," I whisper against her lips.

"Oh, right now?" Her legs slowly fall open for me as I feel her wetness building.

"Just enjoy," I say as I slip my finger inside her slit, dragging the wetness to her ass and circling it. I repeat this process several times before she's breathing heavy, panting, grabbing at my chest as I fuck her pussy with my fingers. I place my thumb at her clit, circling it as my two fingers pump into her. She's so close, I can feel her release building as she grips my fingers. I pull them out, and this time when I drag her wetness back, I press against her asshole. I hear her breathing quicken more and I press harder. I go slow, inching my finger in and out in the smallest increments.

I dip my head down, swirling my tongue around her clit as I push my finger farther into her. She's grabbing my head with one hand, gripping the sheets with the other as I lick her and fuck her asshole with my finger. It doesn't take long before she's coming undone on my lips, her legs shaking and quivering as an orgasm rocks her.

I want to let her rest but looking down her body, seeing her legs splayed open with my finger still inside her ass and her wetness on my tongue, I can't hold back.

"I know you're probably sore, Kate, but I need to fuck you again." I roll over, pulling her on top of me. She doesn't hesitate; she positions herself over me before sliding down my cock.

"Yeah, this"—I struggle to talk as her tits bounce in my face—"this is how I want to die."

THE ROOM IS QUIET. THE STEADY RHYTHM OF KATE'S BREATHING tells me she's either asleep or almost asleep. We've been wrapped in each other's arms for a few hours. I sit up slowly, not wanting to wake her, and reach for my phone in my jeans pocket. It's almost three a.m. I feel movement behind me as the sheets rustle.

"Stay in bed," Kate says, reaching for me. I grab her hand, bringing it to my lips and kissing her fingertips.

"I'm just grabbing water." I walk to the restroom, grabbing a glass of water before walking back to bed and climbing in behind Kate. I pull her back against my chest, burying my nose in the crook of her neck and praying, hoping this isn't the only time I get to fall asleep with her in my arms.

14

KATE

"Good morning and happy Christmas Eve," I roll over, waking to the smell of bacon and coffee.

"Are you serious?" I smile as Damon walks over to the bed with a tray of food. He slowly lowers it to the bed, climbing up to sit next to me.

"Breakfast in bed? You're really trying to butter me up, huh?" I ask, reaching for the cup of coffee.

"Well, your mom made it; I just assembled it." He kisses me on the forehead, something so simple yet so endearing. Is this how life with Damon would be? I wonder, or is this just all still part of the fantasy we've created?

"A girl could get used to this." I wince a little at my confession, but Damon doesn't seem fazed by it.

"So what is the Flowers family tradition for Christmas Eve?" He takes a bite of his toast and washes it down with orange juice.

"Sledding," I say with a mouth full of eggs and bacon.

"Oh yeah?" He looks excited and it makes me smile.

"Yeah, it's kind of a big deal. There's a golf course about three miles away that has this big hill and they open it up to the public. They have hot cocoa and hot dogs and it's a whole big thing. Very Midwest Christmas vibes."

I know to most people it would be lame. Sledding in Illinois isn't exactly thrilling when our biggest hill only has a two percent grade, but we've been doing it since I can remember and it's one of my favorite family traditions.

I see his face fall a little. "Chad coming?" He spits his name out like it's bitter.

"Nope, this is Flowers only so consider yourself extremely lucky I'm letting you tag along." I playfully bump his shoulder. We both finish our breakfast, and I make the bed as Damon returns the tray to the kitchen.

I step into the bathroom, flipping on the water as I brush my teeth. A moment later, Damon walks into the bathroom. He pulls his t-shirt off, his taut muscles rippling with the movement, and I catch myself staring. *God, this man is mouthwatering.*

He doesn't stop with the shirt. He slides his pajama pants down his legs before walking up behind me and kissing my neck.

"Care to join me?" he murmurs like it's normal for us to just be waking up together and going through our routine as a couple. He wraps his arm around my waist, placing his hand on my belly as he plants several more kisses along my neck. My head lulls to the side and I forget I have a toothbrush hanging out of my mouth.

I snap back to reality when I start to choke on the minty toothpaste running down my throat, causing Damon to laugh. I spit it out, rinse, and turn around to smack his bare ass just as he jumps into the shower.

A moment later I'm naked and joining him and a few minutes after that, I'm crying out his name in orgasm.

"OH MY GAAAAAWD!" I SQUEAL AS DAMON AND I CAREEN DOWN THE sledding hill. I'm sitting in the front of the toboggan while Damon's long legs jut out around me. He grips my waist, shouting at me to turn.

I yank the rope, causing us to both fly off the sled to one side, landing in a tangled heap in the snow.

Tears stream down our faces as we laugh hysterically. This is the third time I've made us crash.

"That's it, I'm driving from now on," he says, standing and pulling me to my feet. I stand there in his arms. Our laughter dies down as we stare into each other's eyes. He tilts his head and I mimic his movement, both leaning in as our lips touch.

"Get a room, you lovebirds!" Oliver shouts just as a snowball lands square on our faces.

"Oh, it's on now!" Damon shouts as I step back and try to shake the snow from my hood. He picks up a handful of snow, compacting it into a ball before sending it hurtling at Oliver who dodges it and laughs.

After that, everyone gets in on the snowball fight. Kids and families we've never met have teamed up, creating walls and forts and talking strategy and formation. I haven't laughed this hard in years. I sit back, watching as my family embraces Damon like he belongs, and for a brief moment, I believe it too.

"MERRY CHRISTMAS!" MY DAD SAYS, RAISING A GLASS.

"Merry Christmas!" we all repeat back with glasses raised.

Damon turns to me, clinking his glass of champagne against mine and whispering in my ear, "Merry Christmas, beautiful," before leaning in, his soft lips landing on mine.

"So when do we get to start talking grandbabies, you two?" My mom interrupts our moment, bringing a very much-needed reality check to the moment.

"Mom!" I cough, instantly turning red. I glance over at Damon who looks... calm?

"I guess that depends on your daughter. I'll leave it up to her." He gives me a smile and a wink, reaching over to grab my hand.

What the fuck? This lie is getting a bit too out of hand.

"Well, with the eagerness"—my dad looks over his glasses at both of us—"of their activities, I'm surprised there isn't one on the way already."

Oh. My. God. I cover my face with my hands and sink down into my chair. My face is so red that I'm positive I'll burst into flames at any moment. At least I won't be around anymore to deal with this.

"And on that note, let's open gifts," my mother says, giving my dad a look that says *I told you not to say anything*. "Kate, you're the elf this year."

We bring our wine into the family room where my mother's second Christmas tree sits. This is the one that's decorated with ornaments from our childhood, Chicago Cubs and Bears ornaments and the one we get every year as a family.

When we were kids the presents were piled high and wide, spilling from beneath the tree. But as we've gotten older, the presents have become fewer but more meaningful. I pick them up one at a time, handing a few to Oliver and Erin first. I'm down to one small one left. I bend down and pick it up, opening the tag to see my name.

"Oh, who's this from?" I ask as I spin around right into Damon's arms.

"From me," he says, kissing the top of my head. He grabs my hand and walks me over to the couch to sit beside him.

"Oh, Dennis, sweetheart." My mom fans fake tears as she stares at the ruby bracelet my dad gave her. They play the same game every year—she sends my dad a list of things she wants; he picks a few, and she pretends to be surprised on Christmas Day. I've asked her before if she resents him for it because it's not a surprise or thoughtful but she said it was her idea. After forty Christmases together, it starts to get repetitive and not as much fun to try and surprise each other.

"Open yours, sweetie," my mom says as I clutch the small box in my lap.

I pull the red ribbon off the box and slowly pull off the thick gold wrapping paper. It feels like a shame to destroy such beautiful packaging. I glance at Damon, offering him a shy smile as I lift the lid and see the beautiful Thalia and Melpomene masks in crystal.

"Oh my God, it's beautiful," I say as I pull it out of the box. The ornament has a red ribbon through a small hole on the top. "Thank you," I say to Damon who's smiling at me.

"When I saw it, I immediately thought of you."

I run my fingers over the smooth edges of the crystal and a lump forms in my throat. *He's thoughtful.* This whole time I thought it was just an act but maybe— "I'm so sorry I didn't get you anything." I suddenly feel awful.

"No, don't apologize. I, uh, I already have the most amazing gift I could ask for." He reaches over and squeezes my knee and I think he's done but he slides off the couch and produces another small box from his pocket. I look around nervously but he reaches out and grabs my hand. "I'm so grateful you agreed to be my wife and now, I get to do it right with this."

He opens the box slowly and my hand instinctively shoots to my mouth. There staring back at me is my grandmother's antique wedding ring. I don't think twice; I jump up, tears stinging my eyes as I run up the stairs to my bedroom.

I throw myself on my bed, tears running down my cheeks. How did I get myself into this mess? My parents were right about me; clearly, I can't manage life on my own.

"Kate?" Damon's voice interrupts my thoughts.

"Go away," I say, sniffing as I wipe away the tears.

"Kate, what happened? What's going on?" he asks as he ignores my comment and sits on the bed beside me. He reaches out and touches my leg. I jerk it away, sitting up rapidly.

"Are you fucking serious?" My words sting; he looks like I just slapped him. "This whole thing is a nightmare! It's gone too far." I'm sure my mascara is running down my face but right now, I couldn't give a shit.

"Last Christmas, I thought—I thought that I'd be getting a proposal, a real one from Chad with *that* ring. So it was like salt in the fucking wound when I opened it and saw it staring back at me and it's all just a big fucking lie."

I see his face drop as he hangs his head. "Kate, I had no idea, I'm so sorry. When your mom came to me with the idea, I thought tha—"

"What? When?"

"Two days ago." He looks confused again.

"Are you serious? You've known about this for two days and you didn't say anything to me? You really thought *yeah, this is a good idea*!"

"I don't know. It all happened so fast I got confused and I panicked. I didn't know what to do or what you would want me to do. So I just…"

"Really? Mister always has the perfect answer for everything, mister I can do no wrong, I can fix everything didn't know what to do?" My words are coming out rapid-fire, anger dripping from each one, and I do nothing to stop myself. "You knew!" I say, pointing to him through my tears. "You kept it from me. Just go." He starts to object but I roll back over. "Leave me alone. Please." This time he listens, leaving without another word.

I've nearly cried myself to sleep when I hear the click of the door opening again.

"I said leave me alone." I sniff. When nobody replies, I glance over my shoulder to see my mom walking over to my bed. She sits down next to me and the waterworks start all over again.

"Sweetheart, you don't have to tell me what's wrong, but you do owe that poor man an explanation. He really loves you, honey, but if you've had a change of he—"

"It's not real." I sniff.

"What?"

"It's not real, Mom. We're not engaged; we aren't dating; we're not even friends." Her face is marred with confusion. "He's my boss, Mom."

"Derek?" She gasps, clutching her nonexistent pearls.

"Damon. Derek isn't real. That's the name—it doesn't matter. Damon is just my boss, my asshole, dickbag boss that offered to bring me home for Christmas but being my pretend boyfriend or fiancé was never part of the deal."

"Sweetie, I'm sorry but I am so confused." I let out a sigh and close my eyes briefly before I spend the next several minutes telling her how the plan came about. A few minutes into the story my dad knocks and comes into the room so I have to start over.

"But why, Kate?" my dad asks.

"I'm sure I sound crazy but..." I hesitate.

"It was partly because of Chad and the fact that you guys always seem like you have no faith in me. You acted like once I dropped out of college I was hopeless, and then you were all happy again when I met Chad because he could save me or whatever."

They both stare at me. My dad starts to interrupt me, but I hold up my hand.

"Let me just get this out. Chad isn't the amazing guy you guys think he is. I'm ninety-nine percent positive he cheated on me with Tessa and when we broke up you guys took his side; you acted like my feelings didn't matter." I begin to cry again, and my mom wraps her arms around me.

"I just wanted to feel like I was more important. I just felt like you guys chose him and the fact that I even have to say all this makes me feel like shit." Sobs rack my body and my parents both envelop me in their arms.

They both take turns asking questions. I tell them about how things ended with Chad, that I didn't want to ask them for financial help because I want to pave my own path. I also apologize to them for lying about Damon and not speaking up sooner. My dad half-jokingly threatens to drive over to Chad's house and "handle" him, whatever that means.

"Kate," my mom says, pausing at my door. "I know that it was fake and I know you two have a very rocky history, but that man down there loves you; whether you want to hear it or admit it, he loves you."

15

DAMON

The drive home is mostly silent, only quiet nods when I ask if she wants to stop at Starbucks or needs to use the restroom. She spends the time either staring out the window, sleeping, or pretending to sleep. There are so many things I want to say to her but I know now isn't the time. What I really want to know is if any of it was real for her.

She glances at her phone. We left pretty early from her parents' house and with it only being a three-hour drive, we still have most of the afternoon and evening left.

"Can you drop me at the tow yard?" she asks.

"Oh." What I had hoped would end up being a grand romantic gesture had things not turned sour this week now seems like it's going to go over like a lead balloon. "I, uh— I called and had your car towed last week actually." Out of the corner of my eye I see her head snap in my direction.

"Towed to where?"

"My buddy, Teller, his brother-in-law owns a garage. He said he could get it in and fixed for you, and then he dropped it off at your apartment. The keys are with your office." I grip the steering wheel, fully expecting for this to be the final straw and her to rip my head off.

After her confession to me and her parents about wanting to do things on her own, I can see how this would seem like a patronizing and undermining move on my part, but that wasn't my intention at all. I'm fully prepared to whip that speech out in my defense.

"Oh, thank you." She glances down, fiddling with the seat belt across her lap. "I appreciate it. I'll pay you back. Just send me the bill."

I just nod in the affirmative. Now is not the time for me to stand my ground and insist that she doesn't need to pay me back.

"It was my fault you ended up in the mess you did with it all so it was the least I could do. Again, I'm sorry about that whole thing and how I handled it." This time she nods and then leans back in her seat to stare out the window for the last thirty minutes of the trip.

When I pull up to Kate's building, I unlatch my seat belt and go to reach for the door handle.

"It's okay, I got it," she says, reaching behind to grab her bag. It's silent between us as she hesitates, her hand on the handle. It feels like the air has been sucked from my lungs. I want so badly to reach out and grab her, to pull her to me and tell her these last several days have been the best of my life and that I never want to let her go. I want to tell her that she's beautiful and amazing and dynamic and I know without a doubt that I'm in love with her.

"Thanks for the ride home and the car. I'll see you at work." She gives me a tight-lipped smile before hopping out of the car and hurrying into her building, not turning back.

EVERY MINUTE OF EVERY DAY OF THE LAST THREE DAYS HAVE BEEN torture. The air is tense between Kate and me. I've gone out of my way to give her space, hoping that each new morning pissy, snippy Kate will show up to work, ready to rip my head off. I'd give anything to have that version of Kate right now instead of the quiet, sullen version. The sadness in her eyes is killing me. Even her walk is sad.

"So, got any fun weekend plans?" I ask her, trying to break the ice as she places a stack of files on my desk.

"No, no plans." She clasps her hands together in front of her, her face void of any emotion.

"What about New Year's?" I ask and she shakes her head no with a slight shoulder shrug. I glance past her; the hallway behind her is empty. It's after five so most people have gone home for the evening. I can't take this anymore; I have to do something. "Kate, can you close the door for a moment?"

She stares at me for a brief second, blinking before walking over and shutting the door. I gesture to the chairs in front of my desk and she takes a seat. I stand and begin to pace nervously.

"I know this is unprofessional to do at work, but I feel like I have no choice. I can't stand this"—I gesture with my hands as I try to find the right word—"heaviness between us. I fucked up royally and I know that, Kate. It kills me to know how bad I hurt you and disappointed you and your family."

I walk over to her, crouching down in front of her as I grab her hands in mine.

"If I could take it all back I would, in an instant. I shouldn't have pretended to be something I'm not to you. I shouldn't have lied to your family, and I sure as hell shouldn't have given you your grandmother's ring like that. You have every right to hate me and be mad at me and I don't blame you. I just want you to know how sorry I am. I never meant to hurt you." I shake my head; I'm so ashamed.

I feel Kate's hands stir beneath mine as she wraps hers around mine. I look up to meet her gaze and I see a sympathetic glint in her eyes.

"I'm not mad at you, Damon," she says in a hushed tone. "I mean, I was. I was really pissed, but I understand that you were trying to help, even if it was in a really fucked-up way." She laughs a little and it makes my heart flutter.

"I'm mad at myself more than anything but truthfully I'm just feeling sad for myself. I'm sad that I gave so much time to Chad, even after the breakup. I hate that I didn't stand up for myself; you were right about that. My parents felt awful and apologized. I even spoke to Oliver and explained things to him. They were all so understanding and I wasted so much time being too scared to speak up. So thank you for pushing me to grow a backbone."

I squeeze her hands in mine as I stand up. I'm about to tell her more, that I want more, that I want her, but she stands up and walks to the door. "And don't worry, I'm sure we'll go back to hating each other and hurling insults in no time." I watch as she walks out the door and down the hallway.

I sit back at my desk, contemplating my feelings. I want to tell her how I feel but I also want to tell her about my family. I grab a piece of paper from the printer and a pen and start writing.

When I glance at the clock again, it's going on eight. I pull my phone out, swiping up to open it and going straight to the messages. I click the conversation with Kate and type out a message.

Me: *Hey, thanks again for our talk tonight. Any chance you're up for company?*

I stare at the message then delete it, typing out a new one.

Me: *You've got cups? I'm bringing the wine.*

No, too cheesy. I delete the message, toss my phone on my desk, and run my hands over my face. I lean back in my chair.

"Fuck it," I say, grabbing the letter, my jacket and keys, and walking to the elevator. I hit the button for the parking garage. I'm just going to show up at her place and hope for the best.

I knock impatiently on her door, my heart thudding in my chest. I hear the lock click as the handle turns and the door slowly opens. A confused Kate stares back at me.

"I'm sorry I didn't text first, but I have something I need to get off my chest," I blurt out.

"Oookay, come in I guess." She opens the door and I step inside.

"I wasn't faking it," I say the words and then stare at her as if she knows what I'm saying but her face shows no signs of recognition. "Every time I held your hand or kissed you or made love to you, I meant it, Kate. I wanted those things. I wanted to know what it was like to feel your warm hand in mine." I take a few steps toward her. "I wanted to know what your soft lips felt like against mine." I step even closer, reaching up and running my thumb along her bottom lip. "I desperately wanted to know what your body felt like beneath mine."

She swallows, her eyes studying mine. "Every time you look at me, I feel my chest tighten. Every time you smile it feels like electricity shoots through me."

"Damon," she says, her eyes filling with tears.

"It was real for me, Kate; every second of it was real. You deserve happiness and love, Kate. You deserve so much more than you give yourself credit for." I place a hand on either side of her face. "I'm in love with you," I whisper. The tears that have been gathering in her eyes tumble down her cheeks as she shakes her head. I lean in and kiss her, the tears moistening her lips. I press my forehead against hers and close my eyes. "Tell me you felt it too, Kate. Tell me you meant it. Tell me I mean something to you." I'm begging, pleading, but I don't care.

She reaches her hands up, grasping mine and pulling them away from her face as she steps back. "I'm sorry," she whispers, "I can't do this."

My arms fall and it feels like my heart is in my stomach. I hang my head. I don't say another word. I just reach into my coat pocket, pull out the letter and place it on the counter, then I turn and walk out of her apartment.

16

KATE

He's in love with me? I repeat the words to myself over and over again in my head. I can't even process what just happened. I was so overwhelmed yet scared. I didn't want to just fall into his arms and get swept up in my own emotions. I need to process things, to understand what my own feelings are.

Instead of falling on the floor and sobbing like I did when I let Chad walk out of my life, a small smile spreads across my lips and I reach up and touch them. They're still warm from his kiss. Butterflies dance in my stomach as I close my eyes and hear his words in my head. Then I remember the letter he placed on the counter. My eyes pop open and I reach for it.

I take the letter to the couch, completely unsure of the contents. *Oh God*, I think to myself, what if this letter has some dark secret that will ruin any chance of us being together. I push the fears aside and pull the letter from the envelope.

Dear Kate,

By now you hopefully not only know how truly sorry I am for hurting you and causing you pain, not only this last week but since we've known each other. I've been a selfish, entitled asshole without any regard for your feelings and I cannot express to you how truly sorry I am. I don't deserve your forgiveness; I know that implicitly.

I hope you also know that I love you, truly and deeply. I know that probably seems unlikely given how I've treated you but the truth is, I was insecure and immature and projecting. I knew from the moment my eyes landed on you that I wanted you and I knew within fifteen minutes of speaking with you that you were too good for me. So instead of being a man and being respectful and kind to you, I tortured you because I wanted you so badly and had convinced myself that a woman like you would never fall for me. I hope I'm wrong. I hope that you saw through it all. I hope that you will give me a chance to prove to you that I can be the man you deserve. But even if you don't, I won't stop loving you, but I will respect you and your wishes.

The other thing I wanted to tell you about, the main reason for this letter, is to tell you why I don't celebrate the holidays with my family. I don't have a family anymore. I lost them eight years ago.

When I was twenty-four, I was living here in Chicago. I had this amazing job where I was making five times what any other twenty-four-year-old was making. Life was good but I was bitter and angry at my family. I felt like they never took the time to come visit me in Chicago; they were too comfortable in their life back in Iowa. They hated the city and I felt like they always expected me to be the one to travel to see them. So, one Christmas I just decided I wasn't going home. I didn't tell them why; I didn't even bother telling them at all actually. So they decided to pile in the car and drive here to surprise me. The weather turned on the drive and my parents and younger sister all died in a car crash that night. I'd give anything to go back and tell them why I was hurting, to explain to them that I wanted to feel like I mattered to them still. Instead, I just became angry at them and pulled away. I do blame myself for what happened. I know you're a much better person than me and you'd never let things get that far with your family, but please understand that's why I pushed so hard for you to be open and honest with them about your feelings. Life is so short and unpredictable. Whatever it is you're feeling, say it; whatever you want, go for it.

Thank you for being an amazing friend to me, even when I didn't deserve it. You are the most wonderful person, Kate, and I hope you NEVER doubt that.

All my love,
Damon

I drop the letter onto my lap. My heart breaks into a million pieces for him. I want to run after him and pull him into my arms and tell him it wasn't his fault. I want to tell him that I'm in love with him too, but I know that I need to take the weekend to process things.

I reread the part about why he's been so cruel to me over the last few years. It stings. I thought he hated me. I think back to the bullshit theory our teachers and parents taught us as children—*if boys like you, they tease you and throw rocks at you.* Ugh, what a nonsensical and misogynist crock of shit. I know that if Damon and I do end up together, that's something we'll need to work through. I also sit back and think about my own actions, how I fed into his entitlement and cockiness by constantly belittling him and teasing him right back.

"Oh boy." I sigh as I lie back on the couch. "We need some serious therapy," I mutter, laughing to myself at the insane turn of events that has unfolded this last week.

IT'S MONDAY MORNING AND I FEEL GIDDY TO GET BACK TO THE office. After Damon came over on Friday night, I spent the night thinking about my feelings and what I want in life and a partner. I called my mom and spoke to her for almost three hours, not holding back. I spilled all our dirty laundry and told her my fears and concerns. It felt good to let it all out.

I step off the elevator and walk to my desk, placing my things in my drawer and logging in.

"Morning, Marge, have a nice Christmas?" I ask.

"Well, I ate too much and I'm broke again after shopping for my grandkids. What about you?"

I smile and nod. "Yeah, it was actually a great Christmas. Oh, and thanks again for letting me borrow your skirt and turtleneck," I say, grabbing the freshly dry-cleaned outfit and handing it back to her.

I grab my iPad as I make my way to the kitchen, pouring myself and Damon each a cup of coffee. I knock softly on his office door, waiting for his prompt to enter this time.

"Good morning, sir," I say, placing his coffee on the desk and taking a seat. I pull out my iPad to go over our schedule for the day.

"Good morning." He takes the coffee, eyeing me for a moment. He's nervous. I give him a small smile to ease his worry and I see his shoulders drop a few inches in relief.

The day passes quickly and without event. I can see him stealing glances here and there, probably trying to figure out my mood. I have to admit, it's kind of fun having him on pins and needles all day. I wait until Marge and the rest of the admins leave for the day before walking slowly down the hall to Damon's office. His door is open and I casually lean against the doorframe.

"Hey." My greeting startles him. He looks up from the paper he's holding and drops it onto his desk.

"Hey, yourself." He smiles.

"I wanted to thank you for the letter, for explaining things and being so open with me. I really appreciate it. Truly." He nods.

"Oh, one other thing," I say and his eyes dart back up to mine.

"Yes?" he asks excitedly.

"Would you maybe want to grab dinner or a drink sometime?" I look at my nails, trying to play it supercool.

"Like a date?"

"Yeah, like a date," I say, and a huge smile spreads across his face.

"Absolutely. When?"

"Friday night. We'll talk specifics tomorrow." I smile and walk back to my desk to grab my things and head home.

I've been home barely five minutes when I hear a knock at my door. Instead of looking through the peephole, I swing the door open and see Damon staring back at me.

"I couldn't wait till Friday." His words are rushed as he takes two large steps, closing the distance between us. He kicks the door closed as he grabs my arm and pulls me toward him, our lips crashing against each other.

The kiss is frenzied, his hands pulling at my coat that I've yet to remove. I mirror his actions, pulling his coat down his arms as he walks me farther into my apartment. He removes my coat, then reaching down, he grips the hem of my sweater and pulls it swiftly over my head, peppering kisses from my lips and chin down my neck to my breasts.

"I love you," he says over and over again between kisses. I pull his face back, looking at him.

"I'm in love with you too." He picks me up, our lips finding each other again as our tongues dance together. He carries me to the bedroom, slowly sliding me down his body as his hands roam, pulling at my clothes.

We finally manage to strip each other of every bit of clothing, our naked bodies in a tangled heap on the bed. I'm lying on my back, Damon above me. He sits back, staring down at me as he studies me.

"What?" I ask.

"Are you mine?" I nod my head yes. "Say it," he says, dipping his head down and planting a soft kiss on each nipple. "Say you'll be mine."

"I'm yours," I gasp as his lips wrap around a nipple and suck.

He spends the next hours teasing me, kissing, touching, and licking every inch of my body before making love to me over and over again.

EPILOGUE
DAMON-ONE YEAR LATER...

"Kate, we're going to be late!"

"I said five more minutes, Damon!" she snaps back. I shake my head; this woman is going to drive me crazy or kill me, but I wouldn't have it any other way.

After that night together in her apartment, we haven't looked back. We jumped in with both feet and a seriously amazing therapist. We've not only worked through a lot of our personal issues—me harboring guilt about my family, her worried I'll just be Chad 2.0—but we've grown closer through it all. Kate has finally found her calling, teaching voice and acting classes at a local theater as well as being the production and casting manager. She's got her hands full but she's in her element. I was sad to no longer see her at work every day, but I knew it was for the best in order for her to be truly happy. Plus, it wasn't healthy for us to spend that much time together.

She ended up moving in with me after her lease was up, but then we put my condo on the market and it sold in less than twenty-four hours. We just closed on our own condo in the city.

"Oh!" I hear her yelp followed by a crash. I bound up the stairs to see her kicking over a box.

"Just stubbed my toe for like the millionth time on these fucking boxes!" She shoves a stack of boxes out of the way, throwing me a glare as I laugh.

"I'm sorry, sweetheart. I promise as soon as we are back from your parents' house we will spend the weekend unpacking. We'll have this place all organized." I wrap my arm around her as we walk down the stairs toward the front door. "It will be the perfect way to start the new year."

By the time we're pulling into Kate's parents' house, their driveway is full of cars for the annual Flowers family holiday party. Noticeably absent this year is fuckboy Chad and his cheating partner in crime, Tessa.

We barely get inside before we're swept in warm hugs and holiday wishes. I'm on Laurie's arm, being paraded around to different friends and family for an introduction; some I met last year but most are new faces. I glance around the room and see Kate, holding her new niece in her arms while she coos over her next to Erin and Oliver.

"Everything ready?" I ask Laurie, leaning in to whisper in her ear.

"Absolutely," she says, giving my arm a squeeze before turning to face me. "You be good to her," she says, her eyes full of tears as she stands on her tiptoes to kiss my cheek.

"I'd go to the ends of the earth for her," I say reassuringly.

After the cocktail hour and dinner, some folks have left but most are standing around talking, still sipping on wine or coffee while Christmas music pumps through the in-house speakers.

I see Kate across the great room and make eye contact with her. She smiles, a smile I haven't gotten used to seeing yet. It's genuine and warm, the kind of smile I always wanted from her. I give her a wink and motion with my head for her to follow me.

"Have I seen you here before?" She sidles up beside me, looping her arm through mine as I stand next to the massive decorated spruce in the entryway. I wrap my arms around her, pulling her in for a kiss.

"Dance with me." I grasp her hand, twirling her around and back into my arms. She giggles as we slow dance to Frank Sinatra's voice crooning "Have Yourself a Merry Little Christmas."

When the song ends, I pull her back to the Christmas tree. I stand behind her, wrapping my arms around her as I lean in near her ear.

"You get to choose one item from the tree for your Christmas gift this year." I see her glance up at me, confused.

"The ornaments?"

"Just glance around the tree and see if you see something you like."

"Okaaay," she says, stepping out of my arms and studying the tree. She picks up a beautiful silver Tiffany ornament in the shape of a heart, then looks closer at the inscription and sees our names on it. "Oh my God, this is beautiful. Did you?" she asks and I nod.

"You sure that's the one?" She looks as me suspiciously and puts it back, moving on to look at the others. She moves around the tree, finding another ornament that is a collar with a tiny bell on it and a tag.

"What's this one?" I laugh and reach for it.

"This one is for a kitten. The tag is blank because once you pick one out, we'll have its name engraved on here."

"A kitten?" She squeals and throws her arms around me. "Where?"

"I didn't pick one yet; we'll go to the shelter together and pick one." She jumps up and down and turns back to the tree. One by one she finds the little gifts I've left for her—a personalized luggage tag with two tickets to Italy, her dream vacation destination, a keychain with a picture of us from this past summer—but she hasn't found the last one yet.

"Wait," she says, spinning around to face me. "I only get to choose one?" Her eyes look big and sad.

"Of course not, sweetheart, but there's one left." I spin her back around and move her closer to where it's at.

"I don't see anything—" She freezes as she stares at the twinkle lights glinting off the diamond. "Oh my God." She slowly reaches her hand out and pulls the red ribbon from the tree branch, her grandmother's diamond wedding ring dangling on the end.

I take the ring from her, reaching for her hand and dropping to one knee. This time I'm doing it right.

"Kate Flowers, you're it, baby. Will you marry me?" She nods her head enthusiastically as she jumps into my arms, knocking me over. We laugh on the floor as she peppers my face with kisses and I slide the ring onto her finger.

"It's so beautiful," she whispers as she admires the new setting I had it placed in.

"You are my one and only, Kate. Thank you," I whisper, choking back tears.

"For what?"

"For believing in us and giving me a second chance. Thank you for letting me love you."

This is exactly how I wanted to do it, just the two of us. I stand and pull her to her feet as we continue dancing, the soft glow of the Christmas lights surrounding us and the promise of forever filling us with joy and happiness.

LOVE a good holiday romance? Be sure to read my other Christmas story: *Naughty or Nice*

Dear Santa,
I know I'm supposed to be nice, but this year, I need to be really naughty.
Oh, and I need a BIG favor—Carson Wells, in nothing but a big pretty bow under my Christmas tree.

Xoxo,
Felicity

NAUGHTY OR NICE SNEAK PEEK

***Dear Santa,**
I know I'm supposed to be nice, but this year, I need to be really naughty.
Oh, and I need a BIG favor—Carson Wells, in nothing but a big pretty bow under my Christmas tree.

**Xoxo,
Felicity***

Look, I'm desperate okay.
I've been the kid sister, sidekick, and friend zone queen since I was seven years old,
But this year, that all changes.

Growing up next door to my best friend was pure, wonderful…torture.
From the moment my seven-year-old eyes landed on Carson,
I was head over heels in love.

I tried to wish him to fall in love with me but all it got me was rejection.

Forget feelings and romance this year,
I'm going in for the kill—pure seduction.
After all, Christmas is the time of year to let it all out, right?

I know Santa won't approve but, I'm done being nice. It's time for Carson Wells to see my naughty side once and for all.

CHAPTER ONE
FELICITY

I'm sitting on my bed in my dorm room, cleaning out my desk to start the packing process. Tomorrow, I will be graduating and done with college. The thought excites me to no end. I mean, no more tests, no more term papers, no more early mornings and races to the coffee cart on my way to class. Tomorrow, I will be a college graduate!

As I look around my room that's decorated with pictures of me and my friends from my time at college, I feel a little sad to be putting this chapter of my life behind me. It was a lot of work, but I did have some fun times. At least these last few years I knew what day-to-day life would look like. After tomorrow, I have no idea. It's like a big blank chalkboard. I have no idea what I'm doing other than going back home with my mom after graduation. From there, I get to settle back into my old room while I apply for jobs and figure out my future.

Figure out my future.

Man, I can't even explain how badly those words scare me. I'm terrified that I will get hired on some place only to find out that I don't have what it takes. Then these last few years will have been nothing but a waste. Not only that, but the money that my mom spent on my college is wasted too. Good money that she worked hard for. Money that she could've used to re-roof the house instead of taking out a loan. Guilt eats at me, but it also pushes me forward. I can't fail. I won't fail.

I take a drawer out of my desk and shake it over the empty box on my bed, too lazy to actually go through it and throw shit away. My phone rings and when I see Carson's name flashing on the screen, I drop the drawer onto my bed and answer it as quickly as I can.

"Hey, you," I say, full of energy and excitement.

"Hi, sweetheart. What are you up to?" he asks in his thick, deep, raspy voice. His voice has always sent shivers down my spine. Goosebumps prickle my skin every time I hear it.

"Oh, you know. Cleaning out my desk and packing my whole life into a box. You?"

He ignores my question and instead focuses on me. "That's right. Tomorrow is the big day. Are you nervous?"

I shrug out of habit to getting this question. "I'm not nervous about the concept of graduating, but I am nervous about what comes after it."

"What do you mean? Going back home?"

"Yeah, that and having to figure out the rest of my life. I'm just scared that I'll fail and let everyone down, you know?"

"Not possible."

I snort and that makes him laugh.

"I wouldn't expect *you* to listen to *me*, but you have to know that you've never been able to let any of us down. Not me. Not your mom."

"Well, now I know that isn't true," I tease as I feel my face warm from his compliment.

He laughs. "When have you ever let us down?"

"How about that time that we got hammered and you had to throw me over your shoulder and carry me into the house even though I was puking down your back?"

He laughs at the memory. "That wasn't your proudest moment, but neither of us were let down then either."

"I don't know. I seem to remember a very long, boring conversation with my mother the next day as she forced me to eat the world's greasiest bacon and eggs."

He laughs again and it makes my stomach muscles tighten as need for him floods my entire body. "Actually, I'm pretty proud of you for that. You beat the town drunk at a shots contest. You're my hero. Have I told you that lately?" he teases as his laughter fills my ears.

"Yeah, yeah," I say, not feeling like a hero to anyone. "I didn't accomplish anything that night but getting wasted, dancing on a table, losing my bra somehow, and then puking down your back as you carried me to the house. You shouldn't have picked me up over your shoulder like that. All that pressure on my stomach forced all the alcohol up."

He chuckles. "You lost your bra because you weren't just dancing on that table. You were stripping, or at least attempting to. And I had to pick you up like that. You refused to come in the house."

I gasp. "You never told me that!"

"What? That you refused to come in the house?"

"No, that I was stripping!"

He laughs. "How else would you have lost your bra? You actually tried to recreate that scene in *Flashdance*," he says, the words tumbling out of his mouth in a fit of laughter.

"I don't know. I thought I was about to get lucky with some cute guy or something," I say, but actually, in my messed-up, drunk-out-of-my-mind head, I thought that maybe Carson and I let things get out of hand. That he was the one who took my bra off and I thought that maybe he kept it as a little souvenir.

He laughs harder. "If you think I would've let you go off with some guy when you were that wasted, you have another thing coming."

My face heats up with embarrassment when I think about how everyone was at that party my senior year and how they've all now seen me topless. "Why didn't you stop me?"

"I tried. I did. It was just a little too late. I walked outside by the pool. There was music going and a big crowd gathered around the table. So I walked closer and that's when I saw what everyone was looking at and cheering for. You! You were up there dancing and your shirt was coming off. Then as I was squeezing my way through the crowd to get to you, you saw me, smirked, and started to take your bra off under your shirt, shouting, 'I'm Jennifer Beals!' It's like you were trying to make me lose my mind. You got it off and swung it around your head, then threw it into the crowd. I grabbed you and your bra that you flung on the table shortly after and pulled you out of there."

I shake my head at myself with my eyes closed. Now that he mentions it, the memory resurfaces.

I'm on the table, dancing to the music as a crowd grows around me. I'm drunk out of my mind. My vision is blurring and everything seems to be blending together, but I feel like a superstar up on this table with everyone crowding around me. They're all hooting and hollering and cheering me on.

"Take it off!" someone in the crowd yells and I think, why not?

My hands find the bottom of my shirt and start to pull it off then decide to take my bra off instead. The cheers grow louder as I let the material drop from between my fingers. It falls to my feet on top of the table. I sway my hips from side to side and wiggle my shoulders to make my breasts jiggle. Even more cheers.

Well, I wanted to get Carson's attention. I guess this is one way to do it.

As I dance, I think about how this is something I would never do before. And I mean NEVER!! But ever since Carson left for college a few years ago, a space has been growing between us that was never there before. He's moved on without me. Forgot me. He's got some snobby girlfriend now and I'm jealous in every way possible. Luckily for me, he came home to visit his family and she was too busy to come. I have to make him see that I'm the girl he's supposed to be with. Not her.

"Strip, honey!" someone yells.

Carson comes into view and I see his blue eyes flash angrily to the side at whoever told me to strip. But hey, maybe if I show some skin, he will get a little jealous and realize his true feelings. This is my chance to show him I'm not that nice girl he's always known. I'm a woman now, with needs. I reach behind me and unclasp my bra. The straps fall from my shoulders and Carson's eyes land on mine. I can read the message he's sending me.

Don't you fucking dare.

But I don't listen and he knows that about me. The bra falls and I catch it in one hand by the strap. I spin it around with my hand and let go. It goes flying into the crowd. In the same instant, I feel like I'm falling. But then I look up and see that I haven't fallen. I'm in his arms. My chest pressed to his as he carries me through the crowd and out the back of the privacy fence. He presses my back against the wood and our eyes lock. His are so heated it looks like fire burning within them.

"What do you think you're doing?" he asks, low, quiet.

I wet my lips. "Having fun," I reply.

"You think it's fun to show your body to every drunk guy that begs to see it?"

Wait? He doesn't like it? Usually, from what I can remember right now, he would have been one of those drunk guys out there cheering a girl on. Then he would have pulled her down and taken her up to a room so he could enjoy her himself. I've seen it happen! Why isn't he doing it now? What's so different with me?

"No, I just..."

"Just what, Felicity?" he asks, and it's only now I can see the anger on his face.

"I just wanted to have fun. I wanted you to have fun."

"Watching you degrade yourself isn't what I consider fun, Felicity. You're drunk. I'm taking you home," he says, forcing my shirt back over my head. I have no choice but to put my arms through. When I do, he latches on to one of them, then drags me around the house and to his car.

My eyes open and lock on a picture I still haven't packed. It's sitting on the corner of my desk. His smiling face stares back at me.

"I forgot all about that," I say, embarrassed all over again.

"Ah, it was a long time ago. I'm sure nobody remembers."

"You do," I point out. "That's bad enough."

He laughs. "Just another fun memory I have of you." I can hear his smile.

"Fun memory? Ha! If I remember correctly, you weren't having fun. You were pissed!"

"Hell yeah, I was. All my friends were drooling all over you. You've been mine since you were seven years old. I wasn't going to let them see you like that."

I smile at his overprotectiveness. I'm his? And I have been since we met when I was seven? My heart starts racing with that thought. I'm his. His.

"Anyway," he says, stealing my thoughts. "I thought I'd just give you a call and wish you luck tomorrow."

"You're coming home too, right?"

He doesn't answer.

"Carson Lee Wells, you promised!" I remind him.

He laughs. "I know, I know. And yes, I'm coming home too."

I can finally breathe. I can't imagine going back home and not having him there. "Good, and don't forget, you owe me for missing my graduation."

He chuckles lightly. It's a deep sound that I can feel in my bones. "I promise, I'll show you a good time to make up for it."

Tingles flood my body when I hear about him promising me a good time. I wonder what that could mean. "Okay, I'll see you soon, then."

"See you soon, sweetheart."

"Bye," I say, and I hear the click of his phone hanging up.

I let out a sigh as I get up and move over to my bed. I throw myself back, dreaming of his face. His blue eyes and the way they seem to cut right through me, making my heart skip a beat. The sharpness of his jaw and his defined cheekbones. That little dimple in his chin and the two that appear on his cheeks when he really smiles. They only come out if the smile is genuine. If it's forced, they don't make an appearance. I close my eyes and picture him standing before me. His tall, muscular body is twice the size of mine. I can see myself running my hands through his short dark hair, over his neck and collarbones, over his pecs and down to his narrow waist where I can unfasten his jeans.

Stop! No good can come from this. If Carson wanted you, he had plenty of chances as we were growing up. We met when I was seven and he was ten. We became friends, then teenagers together. We went through the awkward phase together. I stood back and watched him date girl after girl; every time he introduced me as *Felicity, she's like my kid sister*. Every time, it broke my heart because even at seven years old, I was completely in love with him.

I've been waiting for my chance with him. I thought starting college would make him see me as the woman I am and not some little girl who tags along everywhere he goes. I thought that if I showed him how much I had grown that night my senior year, he would finally see. But he didn't. He didn't see anything but a child misbehaving. He rescued me. I only wish I could have done the same for him.

Sleep finds me quickly even though I don't mean to nod off, but the stress of finals has worn me down. Being warm, comfy, and thinking about Carson though, it pulls me into a warm happy place. Our childhood.

"Hi, I'm Felicity," I say, coming to a stop in front of the new boy who just moved in next door.

He looks at me with his brows pulled together. "I'm Carson. Hey, are there any boys in this neighborhood to play with?" he asks as he spins around to pick up his bike that's lying in the grass at my feet.

I shake my head, feeling my pigtails slapping the sides of my head. "Nope, no kids. Just me." I smile proudly, happy that I finally have a friend to play with.

He scoffs. "That figures."

I frown and cross my arms over my chest. "What's that supposed to mean?"

He looks up at me. "How old are you?"

"Seven and a half," I say matter-of-factly. "I'm the oldest and tallest kid in my first grade class."

He laughs and shakes his head. "That's my point. I'm ten. I'm in fourth grade. A fourth grader and a first grader can't play together. I'm too old." With that, he pushes off on his bike and rides away, down the sidewalk.

I sigh, sad to see my new friend leave. Well, I guess he's not exactly my friend yet, but I hope he will be. There's nobody else here to play with. He'll get bored eventually and I'll be there.

With that thought, I smile to myself as I picture his dark hair, blue eyes, and goofy smile with his crooked teeth. As I walk back across the yard to play by myself, I think of him. I wonder if he'll let me count the freckles on his nose. I have thirteen. I bet he has more. I wonder if I can make shapes out of them like I do with the clouds. My freckles aren't close enough together to make anything out of, but he seems to have a lot. If I can look at them long enough, I bet I can see a square or star or maybe even a heart.

If you love a little (or maybe a lot) naughty with your nice during the holidays then continue reading Naughty or Nice and fall in love with Carson and Felicity's delicious romance!

ALSO BY ALEXIS WINTER

Men of Rocky Mountain Series
Claiming Her Forever
A Second Chance at Forever
Always Be My Forever
Only for Forever

Love You Forever Series
The Wrong Brother
Marrying My Best Friend's BFF
Breaking Up with My Boss
My Accidental Forever
The F It List
The Baby Fling

Slade Brothers Series
Billionaire's Unexpected Bride
Off Limits Daddy
Baby Secret
Loves Me NOT
Best Friend's Sister

Grand Lake Colorado Series
A Complete Small-Town Contemporary Romance Collection

Never Too Late Series
Never Too Late: A Complete Contemporary Romance Second Chance Collection

Make Her Mine Series

My Best Friend's Brother

Billionaire With Benefits

My Boss's Sister

My Best Friend's Ex

Best Friend's Baby

Castille Hotel Series

Hate That I Love You

Business & Pleasure

Baby Mistake

Fake It

South Side Boys Series

Bad Boy Protector-Book 1

Fake Boyfriend-Book 2

Brother-in-law's Baby-Book 3

Bad Boy's Baby-Book 4

Mountain Ridge Series

Just Friends: Mountain Ridge Book 1

Protect Me: Mountain Ridge Book 2

Baby Shock: Mountain Ridge Book 3

ALL BOOKS CAN BE READ AS STAND-ALONE READS WITHIN THESE SERIES

ABOUT THE AUTHOR

Alexis Winter is a contemporary romance author who loves to share her steamy stories with the world. She specializes in billionaires, alpha males and the women they love.

If you love to curl up with a good romance book you will certainly enjoy her work. Whether it's a story about an innocent young woman learning about the world or a sassy and fierce heroine who knows what she wants you're sure to enjoy the happily ever afters she provides.

When Alexis isn't writing away furiously, you can find her exploring the Rocky Mountains, traveling, enjoying a glass of wine or petting a cat.

You can find her books on Amazon or at https://www.alexiswinterauthor.com/

Follow Alexis Winter below for access to advanced copies of upcoming releases, fun giveaways and exclusive deals!

Printed in Great Britain
by Amazon